Just Keep Breathing

Tales of Love and Loss
in New York City

Volume 1

David J. Connor

i

Tortuga Press

First Published 2020

All proceeds from this book with be donated
to the World Wildlife Fund.

ACKNOWLEDGEMENTS

To my family and friends for indulging me as I change lanes from academic writing to creative fiction. In particular, my parents for always encouraging me; my brother (British crime novelist Robert Scragg) for sharing his expertise; my longtime friend Sue Pickett in Germany for kindly proofreading this work; Maria José Iribarne, for coordinating of our weekly writers' group in Buenos Aires; Craig Copland (prolific author of Sherlock Holmes novellas) and Carolyn Kerr (author of *An Argentine in my Kitchen*), who talked me through the process of publication. And Gustavo Ruben Gordillo for being Gus and making me smile.

To the Buenos Aires English Writers Group
for supporting each other
in our love and labor of writing

AUTHOR'S PREFACE

This volume is the first in a trilogy featuring fifty-two interconnected short stories of New Yorkers. The number of tales was chosen for two reasons. First, it reflects the weeks in a year, signifying the predictable circularity of time. Second, it symbolizes a deck of playing cards, representing unpredictable situations that involve luck—both good and bad—requiring choices to be made about the hand that's dealt.

When contemplating what it means to be human, one of the things uniting us all is our experiences with love and loss. Not merely limited to a romantic sense, although admittedly, that is an important part of our world. Rather, we know there are many kinds of love we feel—for family members, friends, Gods, pets, idols, places...the list goes on. We also know everything that can be loved, can also be lost—to time, to chance, to change, to death. When this happens, we may experience great distress, disequilibrium in our lives, even disillusionment. And yet we move forward. We keep breathing. The losses fold into ourselves, becoming a part of who we are. We learn from them. And we keep loving.

This trilogy is an exploration of how people make sense of love and loss in their lives. It is set in New York City, a microcosm of the world with an astounding range of human diversity found throughout its five boroughs. The characters in these tales reflect that diversity, mirroring our commonalities in their strengths and frailties, desires and fears, hopes and struggles. It is my own hope that the people in these stories can serve as a prism for us all to reflect upon what makes us who we are.

A NOTE TO THE READER

Given the broad theme of the trilogy, stories range in topic and tone, varying in terms of humor and seriousness. In brief, I have endeavored to cast a wide net to capture human experiences and the emotions they evoke. Because of this, I am compelled to share a trigger warning. The stories of Brian and Tara include incidents of non-consensual sex. Readers who find the content disturbing may choose to omit these chapters.

Table of Contents

Annie

It's not every day you get to kill your husband.

Legally.

Annie sat at the side of the bed, looking at the man she had given her life to. Covered in wires and tubes, surrounded by humming and beeping machines, Jason seemed more like a character in a science fiction film who had been transported through time and space with the promise of a new beginning. Indeed, in such a movie he would be on the threshold of waking up, simply waiting for a chemical injection to revive him.

She hadn't seen him in over six years. He was the picture of health then, one of those middle-aged men whose life became galvanized by the sudden realization of needing more than the safely-plotted parameters of a long marriage. On leaving, Jason had uttered the searing cliché, "It's not you, it's me." As if that was, both, a satisfying reason to, and sufficient consolation for, the unexpected closure of three decades together.

How could he not have foreseen the magnitude of the earthquake he created? That the subsequent devastation of all that Annie knew to be solid would crash to the ground, leaving her buried under the rubble of their previous life? Yet somehow, numb and immobilized, Annie found herself thinking: *Just keep breathing.*

Disbelief that the earthquake had occurred stayed with her for a long time. Month after month, upon waking every morning, Annie hoped it had been a dream. But her body informed her otherwise in the form of an ulcer planted deep in her stomach like a perpetually clenched fist.

1

Back on her feet, Annie experienced unexpected aftershocks that triggered flashbacks; they raised doubts about her own judgment, giving rise to a generalized fear that had stayed with her until the present.

The thought of getting out of bed paralyzed Annie. In recurring dreams, she stood with toes over the rim of a pitch-black abyss that stretched endlessly beneath: a manifestation of feeling unable to trust the ground she walked on.

Annie sometimes found herself wandering aimlessly through the labyrinth of streets, engulfed by the shadows of tall buildings. She caught glimpses of a faceless stranger mirrored in store windows that she knew to be herself.

She had never felt such pain or as powerless.

Annie and Jason had shared everything during their time together. They had supported each other throughout their careers as social workers, rising to high positions within the New York City system. Over the dinner table every night, each helped the other talk through ethical dilemmas, solve professional problems, and debrief national and local news. They chatted about art galleries visited, sports events attended, books read, plays seen, and shared tidbits about how various family members and friends were doing. Jason had not wanted children, and although this once created a rift between them, Annie learned to accept the situation and eventually moved past it. So, they indulged their *wanderlust*, travelling the world together, from Aruba to Zanzibar.

He was everything to Annie. Now, he was no longer there.

At first, she didn't know what to do with the sadness; it penetrated her bones like winter frost, unwilling to leave. Annie knew the intensity of these emotions had to be acknowledged, but also contained. This had been her personal work every day for over six years.

And yet, from the perspective of those closest to her, Annie had successfully rebuilt her life. Focusing with renewed vigor on her job, she gained a promotion and salary increase. In addition, studying for a degree in Fine Art—something she had always wanted to do—Annie had made new friends and produced some of her best paintings to date. After a respectful period of mourning, she'd also met a nice man named Michael and began traveling with him. While cautious, Annie was happy to be with someone again.

However, that in itself, was not without pain. Their first night together, Annie barely slept; she found herself hovering in a state of shallow consciousness. When a light-snoring Michael held her from behind, for a moment, she thought it was her husband. After all, her only association of such intimacy for over three decades had been Jason. That night Annie realized her new relationship was borne from the ashes of another and wondered if these lingering feelings would ever leave.

With time, Annie grew more philosophical, recognizing her experiences to be somewhat universal. There was even a periodic wistfulness that encompassed the acceptance of human fallibility, the finite length of all relationships, and the importance of appreciating the present. Above all, Annie came to know moving forward was inevitable. And while the residue of Jason still stubbornly remained upon her skin, she took comfort in the way time was slowly but surely washing him away.

Until last week, when Annie received the call.

"Mrs. Annie Sutherland?" a male voice inquired with a slight East Indian accent.

"Speaking."

"My name is Doctor Singavi. I'm calling from Beth Israel Hospital. Your husband has been admitted. Can you come

3

over immediately?"

"But I..." she faded off into silence.

"Mr. Jason Sutherland is your husband?" He was surprised by her reaction.

"We are...uh..." She wanted to say divorced but they weren't. As strange as it sounded, they simply hadn't gotten around to doing it.

"I'm very sorry to tell you that he's had a stroke."

"Is he okay?" she managed.

"He's not conscious."

"I'll be there in an hour," she said, calculating cab time in traffic from Riverdale.

On arrival at the hospital ward, she was met by Dr. Singavi, a handsome, middle-aged man, with thick black hair and copper-colored skin. He introduced her to a team of professionals who provided Annie with the prognosis: Jason was not likely to recover. The phrase, "Next to zero" was repeated several times, something to do with pre-existing conditions combined with the nature of the stroke itself which had occurred as Jason was leaving his apartment building.

Annie stood by Jason's bedside looking down on the man she had loved. For a long time, she believed they had been soul mates. And while the very notion of soul mates still appealed to how she *wanted* to view the world, Annie had relegated the idea to myth, reasoning: *how could a soulmate have an expiration date?*

"He has you listed as next of kin, as his wife, with power of attorney," Dr. Singavi informed her. "I know this is terrible news, but we've been in touch with his primary doctor who shared a statement of DNR in your husband's records."

"DNR?" She heard the term before but could not quite place it.

"Do Not Resuscitate."

A sense of calm enveloped Annie. Always a practical person, no time was lost in thanking doctors, and contacting a handful of people, mostly mutual friends. Jason's parents were dead and he, their only child, never stayed in touch with his kin, so his circle of contacts was small. In accepting these obligations, Annie asked for a week to ensure anyone who wished to see Jason one last time could do so. After checking his insurance policy, Dr. Singavi told her it could be done. Annie appreciated his gentle manner and directness; based on their brief exchanges, he struck her as unflappable.

Within the week, five people had visited Jason for the last time, offering Annie condolences as if the last six years hadn't occurred at all. She came every day. Michael once asked to accompany her, but Annie dissuaded him. Part of her new routine included holding Jason's limp hand while talking to him about different periods of their lives together.

That wasn't all. On that first visit to the hospital, she'd taken Jason's wallet and keys. Not fully understanding why, Annie didn't go straight home that day, but instead to Jason's apartment off Union Square. It was smaller than expected, with piles of books and magazines in a living room with minimalist modern furniture.

She found it curious that the apartment held no evidence of another woman. Long ago, friends had once encouraged Annie to date, intimating Jason was already with someone else. If that was the case then, the woman was nowhere to be seen now: no clothes, toiletries, his and hers towels.

5

Annie stood by Jason's bed, as she had at the hospital. Only this one was empty and unmade. It had crumpled pillows sheathed in worn, gray cases. Hesitantly, she reached down and gently pulled a pillow in front of her, pressing it into her face, inhaling deep and long. *Yes, that was him. Jason's smell.* Filling her senses, serving as the key to a closed and long-buried vault, it released countless recollections held hostage in time; now liberated, they moved like a fleet of ghosts through the silent corridors of her memory.

She put the pillow down, aware of that familiar clenching. Fist-in-stomach. But no tears this time.

"Today we'll be doing the procedure," Dr. Singavi informed Annie as she passed him in the hospital hallway.

How many times a day must he deal with these situations? Annie wondered. Over the past week she'd signed reams of paper. *Procedures to extinguish a life,* she'd thought. It was to occur this very afternoon.

For the last time, Annie entered the hospital room, and sat next to Jason. Despite the machines and medicine, over the past week he had atrophied, looking increasingly like a wax effigy. Taking his gray, lifeless hand, harpooned with needles and tubes secured by rosy-pink band-aids, Annie squeezed gently.

"Why do I feel more like an executioner than a bringer of merciful relief?" She asked out loud for no one to hear.

Then, after several minutes of gazing upon his face, she uttered the question that had relentlessly eaten her hollow for years.

"Why did you change?"

The question sat, perched like a watchful bird on the side of Annie's chair, keeping silent vigil.

6

For those last few hours, she and Jason sat hand-in-hand, before Dr. Singavi came into the room and said in a quiet tone, "It's time."

Ravi

Ravi had never seen anything quite like it before in his considerable years as a doctor: Annie's matter-of-factness as her husband lay dying. Also, her detached disposition, as if attending to an acquaintance. Except, perhaps, for the holding of hands, although this, too, had struck him as perhaps perfunctory. He could not stop thinking about her on his drive home to Oyster Bay.

Turning into the driveway, Ravi stopped at the mailbox and pulled out a wad of items held together by a rubber-band, courtesy of his conscientious mailwoman. "More junk," he heard himself say, continuing the drive toward his large, picturesque house surrounded by tall oaks.

Once inside, Ravi slid off his shoes and noticed a hole the size of a dime in one of his socks. He considered darning it, in the frugal way he'd been raised, but then dismissed the idea in favor of throwing the socks away. After all, he had drawers full of unopened socks: Calvin Klein, Giorgio Armani, Michael Kors.

Reaching into the refrigerator, Ravi took out the bottle of New Zealand Sauvignon Blanc he'd opened the previous night and liberally poured a glass. The website from which he'd bought a case had described it as "zippy and grassy," striking him as somewhat quirky for wine. Pulling up a long-legged stool to the breakfast bar, Ravi took a sip, and turned to his mail. As suspected, much of it was predictable and expendable: car insurance rates, new credit card offers, flyers for discounted theater tickets, and requests from various charities.

Then Ravi saw a faded envelope made of cheap paper, on which his name appeared in a familiar style. It was his father's distinctive handwriting, small yet florid, a perfect example of the dying art of calligraphy. Ravi eyed the envelope warily, as

8

if a foreign body had smuggled itself inside the bundle of mail, intruding upon his premises. Plucking a sharp blade from the kitchen drawer, slowly and carefully, he slit open the paper in the same meticulous nature he would a patient's skin and extracted three small, folded sheets. The paper was thin, a pearly translucent membrane, imprinted with blue ink.

Ravi took a large gulp of wine, swooshing it around his mouth several times as if it were mouthwash, before swallowing it all in one gulp. He began to read:

My Dear First Born Son Ravi,

Your mother and I send our love. We miss you. It seems like a long time since we heard from you. Was it over two summers ago? I know a lot has passed between us and we have not always seen eye to eye. Allow me to explain some things that have been on my mind for some time.

When you were born you gave us great hope. From the start, I knew you had something special in you, call it a father's intuition. As you know, I was raised poor but determined to be educated. My family helped me to go to school, and I worked seven days a week driving a taxi so I could get to college. I picked accountancy because I wanted to understand businesses and knew there would always be businesses who needed such men. When I graduated, I secured my first accountancy job working for a British publishing company. I was a good worker and got along with everyone. As time passed, I was happy to move up several ranks, eventually to become chief accountant, coming to know important people in the ex-pat community.

The world changed for me when you were born. Sweet boy with big eyes that everyone loved. I made sure you were in private education. It was a lot of money and you were one of the few Indian children in that school because my bosses vouched for us, saying that we were from an outstanding family. It was my hope that you would be a doctor or a

9

lawyer, not an accountant, so you could help people and make good money. When I came to work in the American Embassy, I knew the Gods were good to our family. I was not the head man, but they relied on me a lot for local knowledge. One day, some men tried to snatch the ambassador's son as he played in the street. I was returning from lunch and witnessed what was happening, so I jumped into the car where he'd been pushed and fought with two men. I have no idea where I got the strength, but I pulled the boy from the car and ran into the gates, locking them fast.

The ambassador was very grateful because the political group that claimed the act were known to sometimes execute their victims. When he asked me what he could do to show his appreciation, I did not hesitate. I said, "Please send my first born son to the United States for school. He is a smart boy, a good boy. He is no trouble." The ambassador told me it would be difficult, but he would try. It took almost a year, but he kept his word. And off you went to high school in Washington DC, a brave boy. You did very well, won scholarships, and were loved by your host family. The next step for you was university, it seemed natural. When you said you wanted to be a doctor, your mother and I were overjoyed. And as the saying goes, the rest is history.

We are so very proud of you, my son. You have had a better life than us, and we are deeply grateful to the Gods for that. All we want is for you to be happy. I know I made you upset at a different point in your life, but it was never intentional. Now you are a mature man. Your mother's eyes are not too good, and her feet swell in the heat making it difficult to walk. We count our blessings daily but know we will not live forever. All we have ever wanted was to see you again, our boy.

When we sent you to America, we thought you'd come back to us. But you were so smart, they wanted to keep you! It has now been over forty years since we saw your face before us. Your three brothers and two sisters have missed *you too. You are an uncle to sixteen beautiful children, and a great uncle to seven more.*

Please come to visit. Do you still have a sweet tooth? Your mother will make gulab jamuns the way you like them.

I close by wishing for you the blessings of the Gods and ask that you find in your heart the desire to make the long journey home.

Your father,

Daljeet Singavi

Ravi put the letter down and reached for his wine glass. His father's ornate handwriting had never changed but the sweet entreaties to return belied his own childhood memories. The obsequious tone, the familiar narrative, and pleadings to visit the family did not convince him.

Instead, Ravi recalled his father's tyrannical ways. The beating. The shaming. The taunting.

Yes, his father had been proud of Ravi's academic prowess, his voracious consumption of books, and ability to figure things out faster than anyone else. But all that changed suddenly when Ravi was fourteen and confided in his teacher that he liked boys more than girls. The teacher stopped by his home that same night and told his parents. They thought Ravi had a devil in him, and tried everything from exorcisms to violent beatings, visiting assorted shamans who performed spells and forced him to drink concoctions made of animal parts and God knows what else until he vomited amid hallucinations while convulsing on the ground. Then, he was left in a room alone for three weeks. Embarrassment had consumed his parents like a plague of locusts. His father bribed the teacher into secrecy with a tidy sum and agonized about what needed to be done with the boy and his sickness that, by its very nature, was against the law.

Soon after he said, "I am planning to send you to America, Ravi, to forget what has happened." In a stern voice he stated, "You will start fresh, study hard, and eventually be able to earn enough money to help the whole family. Such is the responsibility of a first born son." Then he paused for a moment, shifting his vision to look Ravi in the eye. "While you are away, your mother and I will begin looking for a good wife for you."

That was then, and this is now, thought Ravi, gazing at the tightly formed words from halfway around the world lying flat on the counter before him.

The telephone rang, breaking his reverie. Ravi could see on the screen that it was Tony, his husband.

"Hey."

"Are you okay? That sounded like a low 'hey' to me."

"I'm fine," Ravi paused, "Just tired."

"How did it go today?"

"Not too bad. What time will you be home?"

"I have parent-teacher conferences tonight, so I'll be later than usual."

"That's right. I forgot."

"They'll begin showing up any minute. It's usually a big crowd for ninth grade. Just wanted to check in. Gotta go. Love ya."

12

"Love you too," Ravi replied. "Oh, one more thing. On the way home can you pass that Indian restaurant I like and bring home a couple of *gulab jamuns?*"

"Sure. No problem."

Ravi slowly re-read the letter.

Then, with surgical precision, he carefully tore the three sheets into tiny pieces and placed them, like a pile of confetti, on his tidy breakfast bar.

Tony

Ravi seemed distant, even a little distracted, on the phone. It's probably the pressures of work taking their toll. After a dozen years together, there are still things about of him that I don't know about, and perhaps never will. It's not always easy, living with an insular person, but he's worth it.

Two more days to go.

How many came tonight? Let me check my sign-in sheet...

Twenty-seven in all, mainly mothers, some fathers, aunts, and older siblings. Parent-teacher conferences weren't really convenient for many. Most people came from work, looking tired after a long day. Several had babies or small children in tow, probably unable to afford a sitter. But all of them knew the importance of showing up and meeting their kid's teacher. They were more comfortable listening, rather than talking, showing deference to 'maestros' that still exist in many Latino cultures. A few of my kids came with their family members, to translate. It's funny how they avert their eyes when I compliment their work. I can understand it if I share a few shortcomings they need to work on. My formula hasn't changed much over the years:

First, greet them with a big smile and a handshake.

Second, provide three compliments ("Miguel's writing is improving so much...he created a wonderful short play that was performed by the class... he's very creative").

Third, share one major and one moderate area to focus on ("He would do even better if he studied a little more for tests on Fridays...and if he consistently completed his homework every night").

Fourth, encourage the student to share a pre-selected piece of work with their parents.

Fifth, a quick goodbye, and on to the next like a conveyor belt.

I've now taught in this school for over ten years. All in all, that makes it three decades in Queens. I've always enjoyed working with kids. Long ago, I'd like to think I established a reputation of being firm-but-fair. As with any teacher I've known, there have been ups and downs throughout my career but, at the end of the day, I believe the proof's always in the pudding. The contentment of the kids and quality of their work has always been primary. I've loved doing this job.

But things are different now. The relentless pace of teaching for high stakes tests makes it feel like the system cares more about scores than kids. It's wearing me out. I'm not exactly sure what's wrong, but I've always been able to bounce back. It's important to be "present," on the ball—you can't be sloppy. Give the kids an inch, they'll take a mile. As the only black male teacher in this high school, I know I'm valued by administration, the community at large, particularly African-American parents who see in me possibilities for their own sons, so long denied. I've always tried to use a calm approach to resolve difficult situations at work. Now... I feel I've changed. I hate how much schools have become test-prep factories, created by policy-makers who haven't got a clue. If I hear about The Every Student Succeeds Act one more time I'll fucking scream my head off. As I watched that documentary where third graders were crying because they were so stressed about an impending test, it brought me to tears. What have we come to? Kids on medication just to go to school?

I'm not really sure I can do this anymore.

15

It started about a year ago, my mind drifting off when I was at work - it had never happened before. I'd find myself looking out the window at the sky when teaching, instead of at kids. As much as I fought the urge, I kept doing it. Something told me it might be a sign. To change, do something else.

Then I got to thinking...I've had a good run. Thirty years. No major regrets. I was hoping to stay 'til the end of the year, but don't think I can anymore. I'm done. I'll hang in for the rest of the fall semester, so the kids won't experience academic disruption, or feel abandoned. After that, I'm out.

A sudden knock on the classroom door startled Tony. It swung open to reveal a tall, lean woman around forty years old, with dark skin and short, cropped hair.

"Mr. London?" she inquired.

"Yes."

"I know I'm late and you probably want to head out, but I was hoping you'd have a couple of minutes for me."

"Of course," Tony responded, gesturing to a seat placed at an angle parallel to his own.

Shit. I thought I'd done the last one.

He'd purposely positioned the chair as a gesture to promote parity. A desk between himself and parents symbolized distance and power differentials, usually exacerbated by gender, race, and social class. Some colleagues had always busted his chops about this, saying he was taking things too far, but Tony was steadfast in his conviction.

"And you are...?" He extended his hand.

16

"Shantelle Moore." She shook his hand gently. "Jeremy's mother."

"Jeremy who started with us this year?"

The kid with Down Syndrome.

He was a short, heavy-set young man who smiled a lot.

"He's great." Tony said.

"He sure is."

"I know Jeremy's only been here since September," Tony began, "But I see he's done well. He always does his best, produces some good writing—poems, a monologue I remember from last month, and contributes when working in groups..."

"That's so good to know, Mr. London. One reason I'm here is to tell you he loves your class more than anything. Jeremy always talks about you, how you're funny and nice to students."

Tony felt pleased, and a little embarrassed.

"Can I ask where Jeremy was before he came here?"

"His previous school was the Shildrick Institute, all the way up near Bronxville. Jeremy had to spend almost two hours every day on the bus, both, going and coming," she shook her head, disapproving. "It was only for kids with disabilities. They had all sorts together there. Kids with wheelchairs, kids with nurses, autism, mental problems, bad behaviors—you name it."

"I've heard about that place."

"I wanted Jeremy to have school with other kids, typical kids," she continued, "But the Department of Ed's always given me such a hard time. So, I joined a group of parent activists and we brought a lawsuit."

Good for her.

"Well," Tony said, "He's here now and we're happy to have him."

"Better late than never. I was always convinced there would be a better place for him... and you've helped prove I was right."

Her face radiated a quiet satisfaction.

Tony could tell Shantelle wanted to say more.

"Sounds like a tough battle."

"It was," she responded. "You see, even though I was convinced he should be in a school like this, I really didn't know if it would work." She paused, clearly looking for the right words. "Kinda like having answered prayers. When you get what you actually want—how do you respond to it? Know what I mean?"

He nodded.

"I admit I was worried this semester. But now it's more than halfway through and, it..." she broke off, tears washing over her eyes.

"I can only imagine how hard it must have been to get him here..." Tony reached into his desk drawer, removing a box of tissues and placing them next to Shantelle.

"He loves your class, Mr. London," she said again, reaching over and plucking a tissue. "Just loves it. Comes home every night talking about you."

Tony nodded again.

"I wanted to come here today and thank you personally."

He felt blood rise to the surface of his face and hoped she wouldn't see him blush.

"Thank you," he managed.

"I'll not keep you any longer. I know it's late and we both should be on our way home." Shantelle stood up quickly, patting the corner of both eyes with the tissue. "Please excuse me. I didn't mean to get emotional."

"No trouble at all."

"He's come so far," she said, raising her hand goodbye before closing the door.

Jeremy, Jeremy, Jeremy…I never thought twice about having a kid with Down Syndrome in class. Some teachers disagreed with the principal's decision to take him, saying he was mentally retarded and couldn't keep up with the work… All Jeremy needs is to succeed on his own terms. It's not hard to create work for him or adapt what I've planned for the rest of class. I've always hated the word "retarded." What's worse is when teachers use it. Only last week in the faculty cafeteria, a colleague described a student who'd been absent, saying "That kid's retarded."

"Please don't use that word," I asked.

"Why? Most people do."

19

"It's demeaning to people with intellectual disabilities."

"Oh, that's the new politically correct term now, is it—intellectual disabilities?"

"It's seen as a more accurate description."

"A rose by any other name..." he said, making a dismissive hand gesture as if wafting away a fly.

"So, inequalities of race, gender, sexual orientation—thanks to civil rights movements—are now addressed in our language, but people with disabilities are fair game for insults?"

No response.

"Imagine if you were given that label. It would always be the first thing anyone associated with you. And it would stick with you for the duration of your life."

"No need to be so touchy."

"Do you know what people with that label think about it?"

"No."

"The thing they hate the most is the label. It's like a target painted on their t-shirt, always making them an easy mark."

"Maybe you have a point but you can't take on the entire world."

"I know. I'm okay with one person at a time."

"So self-righteous."

"For calling you out when you have kids in your class with that label?"

We walked out of the staff room in different directions. What an asshole.

After Jeremy's mother left, I needed a little time to mull things over.

What is it like for him being in that fool's class? I hate to think of it this way, but it'll prepare the poor kid for lifelong struggles ahead, battling people's views, even so-called 'educated' ones. Imagine taking so long for his mom to get him here. Why are people afraid of working with kids who are a bit different than most?

Anyway, it's getting late, and I have to get home. Ravi will be waiting with dinner and a much-needed glass of wine. What did he ask me to pick up again?

Driving along the highway Tony kept reflecting on his long day. Above all, Jeremy's mother's face kept appearing, saying the words, "He loves your class so much."

Pulling up to the Indian restaurant to get those dessert things whose name he could never pronounce, Tony came to a decision.

Next June's not that far away.

Maybe I'll ride out the year after all.

Shantelle

Who had suggested a Bring Your Pets to Work Day?

No one in the office recalled, but the idea was an immediate hit with everyone except Shantelle. To her, office and pets should be like church and state, kept separate. While she loved animals as much as the next person, the open plan space of a telephone company on East Forty Fourth Street was not a place for them.

That morning, the first to arrive was Daisy, Daniel's golden retriever, affable and portly, with a constantly wagging tail like a windscreen wiper in heavy rain. Next was Mitzi, Jeanne's French poodle, elaborately coiffed and trimmed like a topiary. Then there was Winston, Kendall's British bulldog, as stout as a barrel on four squat legs. Finally, Jimbo, Andy's mutt, a shelter rescue, nondescript and looking somewhat bewildered, as if he'd mistakenly walked into Crufts.

Clenched at the end of taut leashes, the dogs cautiously checked each other out while straining the arm sockets of their loving owners. At first, they sniffed the air in a cursory manner, feigning disinterest while actually scoping the landscape of possibilities. After a few sideways glances, it wasn't long before Winston began nuzzling into Daisy's rear end as if it were a bouquet of pungent roses. Once the ice was broken, Jimbo followed suit, dipping his head below Mitzi's stomach in the general direction of desire. Within seconds they were in a rugby scrum, all flaring nostrils and rolling tongues, poking into intimate parts, while still tethered to their owners.

"They're really enjoying themselves," said Kendall.

"Don't you wish you were a dog sometimes?" asked Daniel.

"Some men are," said Jeanne.

"That's discrimination," Andy protested. "*We* can't say some of *you* are female versions of a dog."

"True," agreed Jeanne, adding, "but some of us are."

"We're skating on thin ice here," Andy responded, "Let's not say anything we'll regret and end up on charges. It's our inaugural event and is supposed to be a happy day!"

Shantelle sat at her desk. While everyone else seemed to be holding or restraining an animal, she continued working. Occasionally her eyes broke away from the computer screen, due to increasing difficulties in tuning out the commotion.

I don't believe this. When did we become a cross between a dog-pound and a pet store?

Then, in came Mamushka, Linda's Siamese cat with wedgewood-blue eyes and sleek, two-tone fur; on seeing the mass of canines, she instantly froze. Daisy's eyes caught those of Mamushka's and she emitted a low growl.

"Linda, she's beautiful," said Daniel. "Why don't you take her to the other side of the office?" It was a directive camouflaged as a question. "Just in case. We don't want any fighting."

"I thought it was just dogs today," Jeanne said.

"That would be Bring Your *Dog* to Work Day," Linda responded, piqued at being minoritized.

As the menagerie expanded around Shantelle, she fixed her eyes on the computer screen again, meticulously checking transactions in corporate accounts. How she wished Adrian, the office manager, hadn't taken the day off, leaving Daniel in charge.

Daniel started all this bullshit. It's breaking health and safety rules. I should've told Adrian before he left and not worried about being branded a party-pooper-killjoy, that stupid phrase Daniel uses for people who don't agree with him.

José entered with an African Gray parrot on his shoulder.

"He's stunning," Daniel trilled.

"This is Earl... as in Earl Gray."

"Oh... clever." Andy nodded with approval.

"Where's his cage?" Kendall inquired.

"By my locker. He likes to be on my shoulder."

"Does he talk?" Jeanne asked, trying to extricate Mitzi from the scrum.

"He can say a few things."

"Such as?"

"'Jesus H. Christ' and 'Holy Shit.' My wife says them all the time."

Shantelle cracked a smile.

That was funny.

Then it struck her.

Look at them, treating their pets like kids. Fussing, talking to them, giving them the best of everything, thinking they've got unconditional love. They have no idea what that is.

24

Her thoughts turned to her son, Jeremy. She'd been more anxious about him than usual since changing schools; the new one was quite different from the old one. Not all of his teachers were understanding, but he was a big fan Mr. London. Worry pressed down on her some days, to the point where her patience wore thin when faced other people's frivolities.

Do half of these people here even know what it's like to care for a child? Why didn't they have Bring Your Child to Work Day like most other places? It would be good for Jeremy.

She watched as several more cats arrived, including a declawed ginger, a black amputee, and a zoned-out ball of grey fur on anxiety meds. There was also a puppy mistaken for dead at birth named Lazarus, a pair of lovebirds called Bonnie and Clyde, and a chameleon who went by the name of Karma.

There'd also been a couple of "accidents."

"It's nothing. Just a squirt," Daniel said, mopping up the small pool Daisy left on the carpet with half a kitchen roll. "She's not incontinent," he insisted. "It's the excitement of new friends."

The goldfish in a clear plastic pencil case was the last straw for Shantelle. A colleague had dutifully done the rounds showing off Goldie Meir before plonking her on a neighboring desk, looking like a silicone breast implant serving as a paperweight. Goldie's slow, steady-moving mouth, making an O shape, and her glassy, unblinking eyes unnerved Shantelle.

Look at these fools. This is wrong. I can't concentrate. Adrian's going to hear about this on Monday.

Stepping away from her desk, Shantelle motioned to Daniel and Kendall, pointing to their dogs, now rutting by the copy machine.

"They're just playing." Daniel dismissed her with a sharp wave of his hand.

"Playing what? Porn stars?" She asked.

Time for a break.

"Smoke," she mouthed silently then gestured with two splayed fingers bouncing off her lips.

"Enjoy," he mouthed back.

Shantelle slipped out of the office and took the elevator downstairs. On exiting the revolving doors, she noticed the familiar faces of the nearby nicotine klatch: these were people in a fleeting kinship, social pariahs on parade, puffing away in all types of weather. But today, Shantelle had the urge to be alone, so she walked in the opposite direction toward the United Nations, heading for the park benches of Tudor City, a few blocks away.

Once there, she sat and lit a cigarette, inhaling deeply, pulling the smoke into her lungs, savoring the swirls inside. The rush, it made her feel alive. Shantelle had always smoked, except during her pregnancy. She'd tried several times to quit, without success. The drive to smoke was simply too strong, eclipsing any rationale she could muster to the contrary. Even the cautionary photographs on cigarette packets left Shantelle unmoved. Brown gums, bloated feet with missing toes, internal organs covered in growths - they didn't matter.

Smoking calmed her down.

Yesterday, additional accounts that Daniel should have taken care of were unexpectedly handed to Shantelle, making her late for Jeremy's parent-teacher conference. When she arrived at the school, most teachers were packing up. Luck was on her side, though, when she'd managed to find Mr. London, Jeremy's favorite teacher. Before entering the room, she'd looked through the classroom door's glass panels to find him staring intensely into space for a long time. She hesitated to go in, feeling like she'd stumbled on a private moment. However, fearing a missed opportunity, Shantelle gave a quick double knock, breaking his trance, and swinging open the door.

"Mr. London?"

"Yes."

She could immediately feel the kindness in his voice. Shantelle had long divided the world into two types of people—those who understood her and Jeremy, and those who didn't. As he gestured for her to take a seat, she knew he understood.

He might not think of himself in this way, but he's an ally.

She'd always considered Jeremy to be a gift. When doctors told her the fetus inside had an extra chromosome, she was puzzled at first. Then, when they explained that he'd be born with Down Syndrome, she didn't care.

The doctors did.

"We strongly suggest you consider terminating the pregnancy. It's usually standard procedure in these circumstances." Ninety percent of fetuses with Down Syndrome, she came to find out, were aborted. On seeing her reticence, one doctor told her, "It would be irresponsible to bring a baby like that into this world."

Shantelle believed in a woman's right to choose. She couldn't understand why doctors thought the lives of children with Down Syndrome didn't matter. How could they possibly know? What about that family at church? And her former neighbor in Brooklyn? Both had kids with Down Syndrome. The kids seemed happy, it was clear their parents loved them.

Until her pregnancy, she'd thought it was Nazi Germany that desired an ideal human race, not twenty-first century America. And while the doctors didn't change her mind, they did sway her husband.

"Why are you insisting on having this baby?" He asked.

"Because we wanted one and now we have one."

"Not this one. Don't I have a say? It'll be too complicated, Shantelle. He'll be teased. He'll go to a special school. People will feel sorry for us."

"This sounds like it's more about you than him."

"Maybe it is. I don't want a kid who'll never grow up to be a real adult, who'll never be independent. Think about him. What will happen when we die?" In a worried tone he continued, "He could bankrupt us with all of his medical expenses."

"You're exaggerating. Kids are born like this every day and they manage. It's part of life."

A few months later, before Jeremy's birth, his father left – he had returned to his hometown of Nashville. Shantelle wasn't too surprised. She knew men were weak.

Jeremy's worth it. He's always been worth it.

Was that a drop of rain she felt on her hand? Shantelle looked to the sky. It was heavy with thick, grey clouds, reminding her of the phrase about every cloud having a silver lining. She felt another drop on her forehead.

Shantelle took a long, final drag from her cigarette before stubbing it out on the metal bench where it left a circular mark.

When Adrian gets back, he's going to know about those damn pets. That little asshole Daniel who thinks butter wouldn't melt in his mouth...Adrian, too, for that matter. Passing me over to leave him in charge?

She stood up, ready to head back.

I'm going to demand a Bring Your Child to Work Day. If Adrian says no, I'll go above both their heads. You can't discriminate like that, putting pets over people. You just can't.

Daniel

When he saw two white eggs behind the plants on his apartment terrace, Daniel stood still: they were luminous, perfectly formed, resting in a bed of twigs and surrounded by a few stray feathers, mostly gray.

How come I never noticed these before? They must've been here for a while.

His eyes turned to the balcony rail, and met those of a plump pigeon, as still as a statue.

"Are you the mama or the papa?" Daniel asked.

The head of the pigeon repeatedly tilted to one side, then the other, and back again, all the while its eyes fixed on Daniel's.

"Look at feisty lil' ol' you! Claiming your territory."

The bird began to pace back and forth along the rail, jerking its head.

"Don't be nervous. I'm gonna let you stay."

Without breaking the gaze, and in slow motion, Daniel retreated to the apartment.

That night, lying on the bed with his golden retriever by his side, Daniel began his ritual conversation with himself.

First things first. I can't let Daisy out on the terrace anymore, so no more quick trips to the bathroom for her. Anyway, it's kind of gross that I even let that habit develop. Lazy really, no excuses... That pigeon's quite a nice specimen. Beautiful green markings go into purple down the neck. And feet. It has two intact feet! Brooklyn pigeons usually have

30

missing toes—was that the right word, toes? Seems more correct than claws. Must be because we use the phrase 'pigeon-toed' for knock-kneed people. Some of them have no real feet, just deformed stumps making them hobble around like old people with arthritis. How did their feet get like that in the first place? Is it pesticides causing foot rot ... or maybe sitting in the bacteria of their poop? Who knows? Anyway, the point is, there's a beautiful bird on my balcony. Probably female because she looks pretty protective. I know my friends will think I'm crazy, especially the ones who call them flying rats, but I don't mind pigeons. Anyway...

Soon, with an arm draped over a gently snoring Daisy, he was asleep.

The next morning, before setting off for work, Daniel looked through the living room window and, craning his neck, saw the same bird from yesterday sitting on the nest. Nearby, perched on the railing, was another pigeon, slightly bigger, and with splashes of brown and white.

"Hey daddy," Daniel said through the glass, by way of introduction. "We're gonna have twins!"

His own love of animals had begun, and been nurtured, in Friday night rituals of watching television with Grandpa Isaac. The amazement shared about the world's natural wonders— from the Serengeti Plains to the South Pacific Seas—still stirred in Daniel. Usually an unemotional man, Grandpa Isaac became teary-eyed when witnessing the vagaries of nature. Daniel recalled one time when a mother cheetah trying to protect her scrawny litter of cubs was killed by lions. The cubs, looking increasingly bewildered as the hungry pride closed in on them, prompted his grandfather to utter, "Poor little bastards. They don't stand a chance."

He and Grandpa reveled in seeing unfamiliar creatures from all over the world—grizzlies and pandas, elephants and dung beetles, tigers and pythons. One of Daniel's favorites

31

were whales with their long, mournful sounds communicating across vast distances.

"Gramps would be proud," he said out loud, imagining approval from the pigeons.

He still missed the old man.

At the telephone company, Daniel told several co-workers about the nest.

"Ugggghhhhh!" said Kendall, "I could never do that. They're dirtier than pigs."

"It's a nice gesture," countered Andy, "Respecting new life brought into the world."

"Wait until you have to clean their shit up!" Jeanne chimed in.

"You might feel different then," said Shantelle.

Two weeks passed without Daniel stepping onto the balcony. Daily, craning his neck and pressing his face against the window, he observed the birds taking turns sitting on the nest. Daniel tried to picture what it must feel like incubating eggs, the great pull of nurturing the unborn, programmed deep into DNA. The responsibility. The care. It was as if a wildlife documentary had materialized at the periphery of his living room.

Daniel only shared his avian observations with Andy, his sole supporter in protecting the nest, regularly whispering updates by the water cooler.

"The mom sits on the nest for ages sometimes. She's there morning, noon, and night...I have to wonder when *she* eats!"

"The dad keeps pacing backwards and forwards, like a nervous father outside of a delivery room."

"There's really not that much poop."

Practicing restraint, Daniel never entered the terrace since the day he'd stumbled on the nest. Then one day, he realized the plants desperately needed watering. It hadn't rained for a while, and many of their leaves had drooped, appearing parched and withered around the edges. Carrying water in an old plastic container with one hand, Daniel gently pushed open the door with the other. The challenge would be providing water to thirsty plants while leaving the nest undisturbed.

I can't support fauna at the neglect of flora.

After only one step on the terrace, he heard a quick, fluttering of wings, and the next thing he knew, mama pigeon had flown right by him and up, up, up into the air. Daddy pigeon was nowhere to be seen.

Oh no! I didn't mean for that to happen.

Looking down at the nest, he saw a fissure in one of the eggs.

Damn! I think she's broken it in panic.

Hurriedly watering the plants, Daniel keenly felt guilt wash over him; regret pulsed through his system like bursts of adrenaline.

This was a mistake. I shouldn't've presumed the birds would be okay with me on the terrace. Now one of the eggs is cracked.

Forcing himself to look at the damage done, Daniel's eyes returned to the nest. To his surprise, the fissure wasn't

33

weeping yolk or albumen. Something darker stirred inside, making the slightest of movements, clearly visible through the crack.

Holy baloney! The baby's coming!

The imagined tragedy was instantly transformed into a joyous occasion.

I'm watching new life! It's coming out of its shell!

Gradually, widening from tiny tremors within, the crack gave way to a beaked ball of pimpled brown flesh with short, straw-colored feathers that were still damp.

Oh my God! I'm seeing it before mama pigeon does! Look at how small and helpless it looks. Where is she? The baby needs to be protected, given food... I'm going inside so she'll come straight back. It must have started hatching, just as I came onto the terrace and she freaked out. Poor thing.

Daniel slipped back into his apartment. Over and over, he replayed the image of the chick emerging, just as he'd seen in countless animal documentaries.

What a strange shape it is, like a little dodo. How could that be?

Mama returned soon after, quickly tucking the chick beneath her like a small cushion, before arranging herself comfortably.

We have a baby!

He clapped his hands together and couldn't wait to tell his friends at work.

Within two days, Daniel noticed another chick had appeared.

Even better!

The parents were now taking shifts to keep them both warm and well-fed. He began researching online and discovered baby pigeons grow fast. They'd soon be quite big - the size but not the weight—of full pigeons, deceptively plump with their fluffy down. He even learned a new word, discovering the stage after chickdom: squab.

It was all proving to be a welcome distraction from work where his colleagues acted weird sometimes. When their boss put Daniel in charge for the Friday he'd be out, Shantelle looked disappointed she hadn't been chosen. Daniel suspected this would happen, but the decision hadn't been his to make, and felt he deserved the trust and responsibility as much as anyone else there. Jeanne was happy, too. She was his favorite colleague, so he didn't expect any attitude from her. He'd been worried about her lately as she looked a little drained, making him think: *What could be done to liven up our office a little?* As Jeanne was a fellow dog lover, she'd likely support the idea of a *Bring Your Pets to Work Day.* When he'd mentioned the possibility to her, the next thing he knew she was telling everyone it was a done deal. They were all enthusiastic, except for Shantelle.

That Friday morning, during the pigeons' change of guard, Daniel was delighted to see the chicks' bobbing heads and searching mouths, wide open in diamond shapes. Both had noticeably filled out, their nascent feathers now a dark yellow matting, covering once bare skin. He'd named them Meryl and Keanu after his favorite actors.

"See you guys later!"

Daniel left for work with a pocketful of doggie treats to satisfy Daisy with through the day. She trotted toward the subway in her shiny new collar and leash, window-wiper tail wagging as usual.

Taking his responsibility seriously, Daniel made sure he arrived at the office early. Anticipating a couple of dogs and maybe a few cats, he figured people would make a fuss of them at first and then settle down to work, pets by their side. He envisioned the day running with minimal distraction, save for the occasional stroke or passing pat.

When they started to arrive one by one, Daniel couldn't believe so many fellow employees had brought their pets. He felt an undeniable air of excitement generated by a genuine, collective love of animals. Yes, as the morning progressed, it had gotten a little loud sometimes but not out of hand. Yes, perhaps it would have been better as a morning *or* afternoon event. And yes, there'd been one or two mishaps. Someone's pet had made a deposit in the reception area without anyone claiming it, obliging Daniel to scoop for a stranger, something he objected to in principle.

All in all, bringing pets wasn't a bad idea. Maybe we could make it an annual event?

He also noticed the only person who had not brought in an animal was Shantelle. Nor was she very receptive to her colleagues' pets, either. In fact, she seemed to be annoyed by the whole thing. He'd counted five smoke breaks throughout the day. Plus, she left early, claiming she'd worked late last night.

Not much of a team player, that one. I'll definitely have to have a word with the boss when he gets back.

Arriving home that night, Daniel went directly into the kitchen to get Daisy a dish of fresh water and a bowl of calcium-fortified pellets. It was then that he saw a hand-written note on the table. Immediately, he knew it was from Jimmy, the building's superintendent. In case of emergencies it was management's policy to have a set of keys to all apartments. They'd happened a couple of times before so Daniel was grateful to have someone on his side when it came

36

to making sure the apartment was fine. He picked up the note and read:

Daniel

Today we had a major leak from an apt. two floors above. It was the central pipeline that cracked and caused water damage to some floors. You were lucky as It only affected your bathroom, flooding it. Also some got onto your terrace. When I was here cleaning up I noticed there was a pigeon's nest so I got rid of it. You might want to rearrange the plants, so they don't come back to the same spot next year.

Sorry for any inconvenience.
Jimmy

Jeanne

Jeanne sat at her kitchen table in the small Chinatown apartment she'd lived in for so long, reflecting on becoming a mother at forty-four.

Funny, to think that all the experiences we've had with others can come back to us at any time during our lives. They're a part of who we are, always shaping us—what we think, why we act the way we do. Even if we're unaware of them, they're always with us.

No one at work had been told yet, but Jeanne knew she'd be showing soon so it would have to be done. Nearby, her dog Mitzi lay curled up on the floor, dozing, worn out from the excitement of participating in *Bring Your Pet to Work Day*. She'd originally suggested the idea to Daniel, and before she knew it, he'd made it his, telling anyone who'd listen. Typical of him. Still, it had worked out well and that's what counted.

Jeanne had found herself thinking about her mother, Heather, a lot recently. What would she have said, what might she have thought, how would she have reacted? Jeanne asked:

Would you have understood?
Would you have approved?
Would you have been happy for me?

Heather had given birth to Jeanne at age sixteen. It was a traumatic experience due to unexpected complications, a great deal of pain, and last-minute surgery. For as long as she could remember Jeanne was told, "Giving birth to you almost killed me."

Heather had been pressured, Jeanne later found out, to give her up at birth. That's what Catholic girls had done in the past. But times had changed, there was no longer a sense of shame hovering around an unmarried mother like a bad smell,

38

making her a pariah within the community. Heather never consider letting go of Jeanne for one second, not even as she writhed in agony before the operation. Jeanne would belong to her: someone to love and care for, to give her a reason to be happy about the future.

Seeing the scan changed everything in Jeanne's world. Placing a hand over where the baby lay within her, recalling how it could fit into the palm her hand - she no longer felt alone.

Is this what you felt as a girl, mother, when you first learned about me?

The first seven years of Jeanne's life were spent sharing a bedroom with her mother under her grandparents' roof in a small town outside of Boise, Idaho. In public, they were often mistaken for sisters because they had the same curly brown hair and a smile that insisted it be returned. She imagined the shame her grandparents must have first felt in a public acknowledgment of under-age premarital sex. Churchgoers whispered the news, thinking themselves a cut above Jeanne's unfortunate family.

A generation of young women in the town were lectured by their parents: "Look what happened to Heather Fields, the disgrace she's brought to her family. You must never let that happen to you."

Of course, they meant "us". Folks in those small places spoke to God from one side of their mouths and, in the same breath, gossiped from the other side. Such towns thrived on the misfortunes of neighbors: everyone had long memories and they were far less forgiving than the God they prayed to.

While somethings had changed, much had not. Heather could take the stares, the whispers, the slights. Once, when her parents told her to drop off a food basket for a church member who was terminally ill, his wife accepted the package at the door.

"I am not letting a sinful woman into our home," she told her emaciated husband who was lying on a makeshift bed in the living room. He watched her unpack the food, wishing he had the strength to articulate, *none of that matters.*

It was the teasing at Jeanne's school that did it. She'd come home upset several times, asking why she didn't have a daddy. At first, Heather explained *special children sometimes only have a mommy, and that was simply fine. A mommy was enough. Jeannie, you're one of those children.* Not long after, things became worse. Jeanne barely ate, and didn't want to go to school at all, saying she was sick with stomach pains. Heather suspected something else, and in the midst of gently questioning Jeanne, tears started to spill down her daughter's face.

"I don't want to go!" sobbed Jeanne, shaking. "I don't want to go!"

The bullying had been going on for months. Several boys and girls were now taunting Jeanne regularly during recess.

"You don't have a daddy."

"My mommy said you're a bastard."

"You're not getting into Heaven."

It was the last remark that terrified Jeanne. All the things she'd learned about Jesus, Mary, angels, the good people. Why couldn't she be let into Heaven? The thought of going to Hell gave her nightmares; she dreamt about being chased by demons as she ran through an endless red labyrinth.

What had her mommy done to make her so different from everybody else at school?

40

Heather decided enough was enough. It was one thing for her to bear the perpetual brunt of wanting to keep her child. It was another for her child to be constantly terrorized by her peers.

So, she left town, taking Jeanne to New York City, a place that would become their home for life. After moving into a tiny apartment off the Bowery, Jeanne went to school with children of different races, religions, and families. Everything felt right.

It must have been so hard for you.

Through the kitchen doorway, Jeanne could see the photograph she'd taken of Heather, the one where she's wearing an orange hat, looking at her from the glass cabinet. It was part of a class project Jeanne did as a freshman undergrad, the life study of a family member. Heather was in her mid-30s then.

But we made it.

Jeanne never knew who her father was. She'd asked several times over her life, but Heather refused to say anything. For several years, it had stirred bad blood between them. Although they never stopped speaking to one another, the knowledge Jeanne was denied hung like a gauze sheet between them, preventing them from fully seeing each other.

"It's not fair," Jeanne insisted. "I have the right to know where I'm from."

Heather always shook her head.

"Just be happy you're here. And we have each other." Adding with certitude, "We'll always have each other."

But the feeling of being robbed had consumed Jeanne most of her life. Might she get to know, and even meet her father one day? Did she have half-brothers and sisters? For years, she imagined her father in the form of a clandestine high school romance. She'd fantasized about how much he'd love her, how he'd say keeping it quiet was the biggest mistake of his life and ask, could she ever find it in her heart to forgive him? With the same intensity, Jeanne despised herself for these romantic yearnings, fairy story reunions, and unlimited mercy all around. She counterbalanced such thoughts with possibilities of rape. Could the same schoolboy previously imagined still be the one, but more conniving and sinister? A neighbor? A friend's father? A teacher? It was all a morass from which she couldn't escape. Rather, she resigned herself to the paradoxical presence of absence, and absence of presence, always carried within.

I don't blame you.

Jeanne continued to look in the direction of her mother's photograph.

You had a right. You had your reasons. I'm sorry I gave you a difficult time.

She also felt robbed in a different way, when thinking of the words, "We'll always have each other," because Heather didn't make it to the age Jeanne was now. What started as a small lump had rapidly metastasized, and the disease eclipsed her mother with a speed that stunned them both. As Jeanne expected, there were no dramatic deathbed confessions of paternity. Still, she felt disappointed that Heather took the secret with her as she floated away on that morphine cloud.

Never did Jeanne think she'd be in a similar situation.

What will I tell my child?

Jeanne had been married in her early twenties to Rafael. It was a college romance that, with the wisdom of hindsight, she realized should have remained as such. At first, she was crazy about Rafael, in disbelief at how he was everything she'd always wanted. But Jeanne soon found out her husband had an elusive side, always remaining beyond her reach. Worst of all, an incident occurred that changed how she thought about him altogether. When the marriage dissolved, Jeanne had soldiered through various relationships, some long-term, some short, never experiencing the desire to spend life with any one man. During the same time, she'd tried a range of employment opportunities: receptionist, dental hygienist, and chef, before finally settling into the accounts department of a telephone company. Stable, good benefits, if unexciting.

Then out of the blue, she wanted to have a baby. The thought consumed Jeanne day and night, as if her life depended on it. Until then, she'd had no desire to bring a child into the world. Now, it was all she could think of.

The plan to conceive a baby had to be clean, uncomplicated. She wanted it within her control, without legal threats of paternal rights or high fees for in vitro fertilization. There'd be small risks, of course, such as contracting a sexual disease. Jeanne had already began taking PrEP to prevent HIV and felt confident in weighing her choice of suitors. Having saved roll-over vacation time for a while, she surprised office colleagues by taking off for a three week vacation to Italy.

In Sicily she found a perfect beach, lined with cheerful bistros and friendly bars. By day, Jeanne lay relaxing on a lounge chair perched above the hot sand, covered in sunblock, deepening her tan. In the evening, as the sun waned and cloudless, porcelain-blue skies transitioned to a blaze of orange, Jeanne sat in open air cafés, sunglasses strategically placed on the top of her forehead as she watched the crowd pass by.

An attractive woman by all accounts, Jeanne's brown curly hair and return-to-sender smile had remained constant over time. Wearing a coral red bikini, partially discernible through a translucent beach wrap, Jeanne gazed at the steady flow of people.

The routine in motion:

Step one: It was surprisingly easy to make initial eye contact.

Step two: A backward glance from the targeted party was met with fixed eyes and the hint of smiles on both sides.

Step three: A pause that often varied in length of time, yet always signified the verification of mutual interest.

Step four: Once interest was confirmed and established, being receptive to a stranger's approach and a *buona sera*.

Step five: Jeanne led the way from there.

Sometimes the men walked on, perhaps to meet up with their wives and girlfriends. But many did not.

Jeanne was never surer of anything in her life.

The men who had decided to pursue her were handsome: bold jawlines, good teeth, muscular thighs, and thick heads of hair. All in all, there were twelve that passed the test during that careful, carefree time. The same number as Jesus' disciples, she thought on the flight home and, for fun, visualized them in a tableau of Leonardo's Last Supper. She would always remember their faces this way, as their names had washed out with the morning tide.

Mission accomplished; she was all set.

As Jeanne sat at the kitchen table, her mother's voice entered her thoughts, soothing her like a cup of warm milk.

"The future will take care of itself," she heard Heather say.

44

Yes, the future will take care of itself.

Jeanne smiled at her mother's photograph taken all those years ago.

I'll tell them on Monday.

Rafael

He carefully held the strip of four black and white photographs, gently pinched between thumb and forefinger, as if they were an ancient document. The man wore a baseball cap and the woman large, rounded sunglasses perched midway on her nose. In the first frame, they smiled, the picture of normalcy. The others were filled with exaggerated expressions feigning surprise, outrage, and mock horror. Happy times.

Where was that photo booth? Some Jersey Shore boardwalk or fun fair? Maybe Asbury Park or Atlantic City?

Rafael couldn't justify why he kept the strip of photographs, other than they were simply artifacts of his life, along with vinyl albums and yellowed concert tickets, residing on the top shelf of his wardrobe.

Maybe I should throw out these shoeboxes filled with old stuff and use the shelf for something else?

It had been almost twenty years since his divorce from Jeanne.

They'd met in an *Introduction to Photography* class during freshman year at Cooper Union. He noticed her on the first day, and she, him. A degree of shyness on both sides meant they didn't have a real conversation until mid-semester. Paired up for a "walk about" assignment in an unfamiliar neighborhood, they were charged with capturing Greenpoint in distinctly different ways. This was to be achieved, in part, through a constant conversation exploring subject matter, composition, and color, discussing pros and cons of potential choices.

Rafael liked Jeanne's eye for detail. She had the knack of noticing so many things he missed. An ornate cornice of a

46

decaying building; the metal latticework of a park bench; a pile of garbage reflected in a puddle. Viewed together, they portrayed a neighborhood in slivers of texture, light, and form. Rafael, in contrast, described himself as a "big picture guy," clicking images of entire streets receding into the distance, swaths of landscaped parks, deserted warehouses, and jagged cityscapes. In presenting the project to peers, the professor told Jeanne and Rafael their styles were complementary, perfectly illustrating how two people can view the same phenomenon in a completely different manner.

They moved into a studio apartment and became inseparable. Both were eager to prove themselves adults by leaving the scrutiny and security of their parents' homes behind, downplaying how the families they sought escape from still funded their education. Showing up at Heather's was part of a weekend routine where they enjoyed a hearty meal of comfort food with mac and cheese being their favorite.

It was during these Sunday visits that Rafael found himself noticing Heather more and more. She had such beautiful curly brown hair reaching halfway down her back, which she occasionally pushed behind her shoulders with a quick hand. Heather looked so much like Jeanne. The same frame, similar shaped face, and those eyes. Their laughter sounded interchangeable. Even their voices, to a degree, with Heather's a shade deeper, more relaxing.

Rafael dismissed his interest as something natural. After all, the women were remarkably similar, and not too far apart in age, reasoning—if he were patient—these feelings would pass. Still, framing it as mere curiosity, Rafael asked questions of friends who'd been with older women.

Thoughts about Heather didn't go away. They intensified.

He was disappointed when Jeanne changed her mind about their Sunday visit, or Heather postponed due to a cold. When they did go, Rafael cautioned himself not to look too long or too hard as Heather tiptoed, reaching for the best plates tucked safely on a high shelf. By doing so, she inadvertently firmed her calf muscles, making them curve gently in a way that made Rafael want to reach out and touch them. When serving the food, he watched how Heather's slender fingers wrapped around the serving spoon, the suggestion of veins in the perfect back of her hand. Rafael trained himself to smile innocuously if he felt his gaze upon Jeanne's mother lasted a millisecond too long.

He knew it was wrong but couldn't stop himself.

She'd entered his fantasies now. As Jeanne lay sleeping at night, Rafael regularly conjured up Heather in numerous situations, always focusing on how it would all begin. Running into her unexpectedly somewhere random as rain started, offering to share his umbrella, aware of her slight shoulders quaking against his. Sitting in a cramped restaurant, feeling Heather's thigh brush on his leg and remain there. In her apartment, cleaning up after dinner, washing and drying plates, Heather passing them for him to place on the high shelf. Fingers accidentally brushing, but then touching consciously, first briefly, then slightly longer, until his hand finally rested on hers and their eyes met, forbidden pleasure trumping shame.

Rafael knew it would never happen and, after taking his sophomore class in psychology, psychoanalyzed himself as best he could, wanting to know why humans want things they know they can't have. He realized Freudians would readily diagnose the transference of an Oedipus Complex. In other words, because he secretly yearned for his own mother and couldn't have her, he'd fixated upon someone else's. But, no matter how interesting Rafael found Freud's phallocentric ideas, they were, from a historical perspective, outdated, even silly. So, he cast himself into his own category, as yet unnamed.

It was Jeanne Rafael loved and wanted to marry, but Heather he desired.

Once their knot was tied, he'd optimistically hoped the seriousness of vows and legalized status would help mitigate the attraction to his now mother-in-law. The simple passage of time, Rafael reasoned, would melt it away. Instead, it became worse. He now pictured Heather when making love to Jeanne. Not entirely immune from feelings of guilt, at times Rafael cringed inwardly at his imaginings. Yet the thought of being with Heather always overpowered any psychological screens he erected.

He didn't know why but his contradictory thoughts were reconciled by imagining making love to both women at the same time, resulting in long, creative sessions that left him and Jeanne deeply fulfilled. Rafael rationalized:

If I only imagine it, and don't actually act on it, is it really that bad? After all, we all have the same capacity for imagination. Do I know what is going on in Jeanne's head when we're fucking? Who might she think my tongue belongs to—her Spanish professor? Doctor? The waiter last night? Johnny Depp?

And then the incident happened.

On his daily walk toward New York University, where he studying for a master's degree in Psychology, Rafael passed by his mother-in-law on a busy street.

"Heather?" he called out, noticing she was looking down.

When she turned toward him, her eyes were pink and swollen.

"What's the matter?"

She couldn't respond, her gaze returning to the ground.

49

Rafael moved closer and placed his arms around her, holding her close. Whatever had happened, she was in shock.

"Let me take you home in a taxi," he said.

She nodded, wordless.

Once in her apartment, Heather sat hunched on the sofa crying ceaselessly, tears deflating her small frame like air from a punctured balloon. Rafael had never seen her so upset.

"Heather, what is it?" He implored, now shaken himself.

Moving her head from side to side, she continued looking at the floor.

"Whatever it is, we can figure it out."

"Hold me," she whispered, barely audible.

Rafael sat next to her, placing his arm around her shoulder.

"Tell me," he gently persisted, adding "You can trust me."

"I can't." Her voice cracked. "I can't tell you."

He was at a loss for words and didn't know what to do.

"Can you lie with me on the bed for a little while?" she asked feebly.

"Of course."

Rafael led her to the bed where she lay on her side. Easing behind her, he molded himself to her trembling frame and tentatively placed his arm around her.

"Thank you," she whispered.

Within minutes, he heard the steady breathing of sleep.

Lying there with his nose brushing Heather's curls, and his thighs scooped behind her legs, Rafael discerned a faint smell of perfume. Beneath his arm, he felt her ribs rise and fall, rise and fall. He was seized by an overpowering feeling of tenderness for Heather. Although not yet knowing the source of her pain, he'd begun to feel it. Forcing himself to stay awake, Rafael remained in place, ready to reassure Heather that she wasn't alone.

"Jeanne?"

"Raf? Where are you?"

"I'm calling from your mother's."

"Mom's?"

"I think you should come over right away."

"Is everything okay?" Jeanne asked, concerned.

"Is Mom okay?"

"I don't think so."

He shared what had happened that afternoon, substituting the part of his lying on the bed with sitting on the living room sofa as Heather slept peacefully.

"Why didn't you call me immediately?"

"I didn't know what to do," he said. "Your mom was so upset. All I could do was think of getting her home and calming her down. She's been sleeping for a couple of hours

51

now. I guess I was afraid she'd wake up the same way and wanted to make sure she was okay. She won't talk about what's making her upset."

"I'll be there soon."

When Jeanne arrived, she tiptoed into the bedroom to find Heather curved in the shape of a question mark, still in a deep sleep.

What could it have been that had made her so upset?

Observing Heather's peaceful face, Jeanne noticed the pillow behind her. It had a slightly hollowed out shape, as if a head had rested there. A closer look at the bedcovers beneath the pillow showed part of them bunched and wrinkled. The pit of Jeanne's stomach registered these observations as rapid, unexpected blows that she bore in silence.

That night, opening a bottle of whisky to calm her nerves, Heather shared the news with them of her diagnosis. And in a strange way, that's when it all began, the unravelling. Jeanne needed to prioritize her mother who'd soon begin to waste away. Each passing week left Heather looking increasingly malnourished. Pallid skin stretched across protruding bones, making her look corpse-like while still living. Rafael looked on in a curious form of passivity seeing Heather's skeleton emerge from the contours of what he'd desired for so long.

As Rafael put the photo booth strip back into the shoebox, he noticed another picture. It was of a smiling Heather in an orange hat, taken by Jeanne, one of her favorites from that first class together. He picked it up and stood looking at the face he'd never quite forgotten. Leaving Jeanne's photo on a nearby table, he placed the top back onto the shoebox, returning it to its shelf.

Maybe I'll keep these things. Part of my time capsule.

Unsure of what had motived him to browse in the first place, he picked up Jeanne's photo and slipped it into his wallet.

Rafael had maintained his interest in psychology, meeting his second wife in their doctoral program. Upon discovering her mother had died years before, he gave an inward sigh of relief, fearful of a potential pattern. Studying for his future profession, Rafael had learned there were all kinds of elements within the human psyche. Indeed, each person was a universe, with some parts best left unknown.

Jeez. Look at the time. Gotta get to work.

He began the short walk up Sixth Avenue to his private practice. Rafael's first appointment of the day was with a new client. Strolling along, he prepared to do what he loved to do— enter another brand-new universe. Even the parts better left unknown.

Brian

Never thought I'd be doing this. Waiting for my shrink.

It's not too late to change my mind, pull out.

I owe it to Joe to at least try.

Brian had been dating Joe for six months. It started by surprise—as many relationships do—because both weren't looking for one. They'd met in a bar one Sunday afternoon, to celebrate a mutual friend's thirtieth birthday. After several rounds of drinks, the group went to a nearby Thai restaurant and Brian found himself sitting next to Joe. As plates were passed around heaped with pad thai, spicy noodle, and red curried vegetables, they compared notes on how items tasted.

"I love the flavor of lemongrass," said Joe, "That limey taste that cleans the mouth."

"Me too," shared Brian. "Let's order a plate of green papaya salad."

It started slow. Short exchanges via email grew into longer telephone conversations that developed into coffee dates. Their first dinner together in an Italian restaurant led to a second. Then, three weeks to the day after their green papaya salad, Joe invited Brian for a meal at his apartment. He spent the night. The following weekend Brian reciprocated, and Joe stayed the weekend. Since then, it was most nights, based on who'd be traveling, and who'd be cooking.

On entering Rafael's office, Brian found it more modern than he'd expected. The gunmetal gray walls complemented chrome and black leather furniture. There were no photographs, and only a small, pea-green cactus indicating signs of life. A sudden feeling of claustrophobia made him want to turn around and run.

54

Stay, stay. You're made it this far.

"Have you ever been to therapy before?" began Rafael.

"No, I haven't."

"Well...we have about an hour, and if you're satisfied that the time spent together is useful, we can schedule you for a weekly visit. If I recall from our initial telephone conversation, you said you'd been struggling with anxiety?"

"That's right."

"So, tell me a little bit more about that."

"I've started a relationship. With a man. I'm gay by the way," began Brian. "Your services came highly recommended by the LGBTQ Center as an ally who specializes in all kinds of relationships."

"Yes," encouraged Rafael.

"My partner doesn't know that I'm HIV positive," Brian shared, "I seem to have some sort of block that prevents me from telling him."

The conversation that followed—for that is what it felt like to Brian, and what Rafael aspired to provide—focused on the possible reasons for the blockage. Brian had been afraid to enter a relationship for some time. He'd never told anyone, best friends, or family members, about his HIV status. Nor did he feel the need to discuss his status with partners to date, be they holiday flings, one-night stands, or friends with benefits. Without fail, condoms were always used. But now, despite his fears, Brian knew deep down he wanted a relationship more than anything.

55

"It's time to wind down a little," Rafael said, making sure Brian had a few minutes to transition from wherever his thoughts had been, and return to his current reality. "I think you're right to address the issues that you raised. Would you like to schedule a session for next week?"

"Yes," said Brian. He surprised himself for having been so forthcoming.

If not here, then where?

Rafael was intrigued. His radar registered layers in Brian that could be excavated. The following couple of sessions helped Rafael to better understand Brian's background. Born upstate in Rochester, a once prosperous city that slipped into economic decline, Brian headed to New York City with its promise of work. Family members supported his choices and were fine with him being gay, but didn't like the idea of him living alone, and wanted to see him settle down with someone nice.

It was in the fifth session Brian volunteered:

"I think I want to tell you how I came to have HIV."

Rafael had never thought of initiating the conversation. Some of his clients with HIV found the idea irrelevant, not knowing from whom the disease was contracted. Occasionally, a client had been infected by their partner who genuinely had no idea of their own status. In some cases, they did. Either way, these circumstances were complicated to navigate. Other men and women had been betrayed by straying partners not using adequate protection. Regardless, every case required a different approach, as each possessed complexities that were unpredictable, even unresolvable, other than for the acceptance of human frailties and failings.

"It must be important to you," Rafael said.

"It is," Brian responded quietly. "I haven't told anyone before."

"Thank you for trusting me with your story, then."

"It was an ordinary weekday night," he began. "I'd finished working in the store and decided to go out for a drink with my friend Mateo. Only, something came up, and he bailed on me. Bummer, I thought. Because I'd looked forward to going out all day...so I decided to go solo. I hadn't been to this particular bar—The Oasis—for a couple of years. It was a little fancy, in a townhouse on the Upper East Side. It had several rooms, one that was very cruisy, a lounge, and one with a piano. I was surprised how crowded the place was that night, and decided I'd stay where the piano was... The pianist accommodated requests as best as he could, and people sang their favorite show tunes. It's usually not my kind of thing, but I can appreciate the campy side of it all. What I enjoy are the singers' voices. Most are waiters on their night off. They live for belting out *I'm Gonna Wash That Man Right Outta My Hair* or *Don't Cry for Me Argentina*... Anyway, I'd had a couple of beers before deciding to go to the lounge area and sit at the bar. That way I could see what was going on through the mirrors on the walls. I remember the song *Don't Leave Me This Way* was playing, and there was a Dolly Parton special on the TV screens with the sound muted... Then a guy asked, 'Is this seat taken?' 'Help yourself,' I said. He was about my height, casually dressed, kinda nondescript looking, but with a friendly manner. A conversation began over a bowl of potato chips the bartender had placed between us. 'Do these taste a little stale to you?' he asked, pulling an exaggerated face. 'Kind of,' I said to him. It was true. We got chatting about a few different things—music, movies, other bars in town. He told me his name was Marcus and offered to buy me a drink."

Brian paused for several moments. Rafael waited until he was ready.

"He ordered me another beer and we continued to chat. The next thing I knew I was feeling really, really sleepy... I couldn't keep my eyes open. I remember thinking, *I'm so tired. I need to go to bed.* Then it all became a blur. I could see the bartender looking concerned, saying in slow motion, 'He needs to go home.' And Marcus replying, 'We're friends. I'll take him, I know where he lives.' 'He knows where I live?' I could hear myself think but couldn't open my mouth to speak. Coat on. My arm over his shoulder. The steps outside. Wallet pulled from my pocket. Marcus reading the address from my driver's license. The taxi. Lights streaking by on Lexington, I think, because I vaguely remember passing Bloomingdales... And the sound of car horns—everything so fast outside, everything slow motion inside. Falling asleep several times. Waking up for a second. The car jolting. Feeling sick. Being dragged out the cab. Propped up while Marcus fumbled with the keys, eventually getting them to turn. Still couldn't speak, except to slur, half stumbling, half being dragged along the hallway. Pushed onto the bed. My belt, unfastened. Rolled face down... the feel of my jeans and underwear pulled roughly down over my legs. Thinking - *this shouldn't be happening...this shouldn't be happening* - over and over. But unable to move, unable to speak. What I do remember is hearing a strange noise. I hadn't realized right away but it was me trying to scream. In my head I was shouting but it came out as a low groan... I felt so weak. Then he climbed on top. His weight, heavy, he was heavy. Pushing inside of me. Pain. Moving fast. That's all I could feel before passing out, thinking: *No, this isn't happening. It can't be happening.*"

Brian sat silent for a while.

"You've shared a lot. Would you like to take a breath? Reflect on what's been said?"

"I'm not finished," responded Brian in a low voice. "I want to finish."

"Whatever you prefer."

"I woke up the next day around midday. I knew immediately what had happened and wanted to be sick. My anus hurt. As I pulled myself upright, there were splashes of blood on the sheets. I sat at the edge of the bed, retching. Nothing came up. I was shaking so much; afraid I wouldn't be able to stand. I found by steadying myself against the wall, I could make it to the bathroom. I had to take a shower. That's all I could think of, I had to take a shower."

Brian stared at his hands, now balled into fists.

"I stayed in the shower a long, long time, not sure what to do. I know it sounds stupid, but I kept thinking that it was somehow my fault. If I hadn't gone for a drink alone. If I'd had one beer and came home. But I had a few, and maybe was too friendly..." He trailed off.

"It wasn't your fault," Rafael said softly. "You were raped."

"I know."

"Did you tell the police? File a report?"

"No. I feel like a coward," he said, sounding defeated. "I didn't have it in me to face the police, the questions. I didn't want to have them prodding and swabbing." He paused, raising his head to look at Rafael square in the eyes. Brian paused again, attempting to compose himself.

"Sometimes I lie awake at night wondering if he's out there doing the same thing." Then adding, "If he is, then that makes me responsible."

"For what?"

"If he's doing it to other people."

"First, you're not a coward," Rafael countered. "You're brave. To survive an experience that most people will never have to suffer – it's beyond their imaginations. Second, you're not responsible for his actions." He waited a moment. "It does sound, perhaps, given your concern for others, that you wish you'd gone to the police."

"I do wish I'd gone. Do you think it's too late to go now? "

"No, I don't."

"I'm still afraid."

"Would you like me to come with you?"

"You'd do that?"

"Yes."

"Then I would."

In the sessions that ensued, Rafael and Brian shared perspectives of their visit to the police station later that day. Once Brian's experience had been discussed with two members of the police, one male and one female, it was declared a "case" and referred to the Special Victim's Unit. In turn, the specially trained detectives assigned to the unit had been understanding and direct, conveying the importance of Brian's decision, yet alerting him to how delayed reporting of incidents meant they'd have less to work with. They also visited his apartment, where he described what happened and where, acknowledging that any evidence was now long gone. Brian was assigned a case manager and encouraged to attend specialist counseling.

Several weeks later Brian told Rafael, "I had to build myself up to go for the HIV test. I had it in the back of my mind that I was okay. Talk about misplaced optimism. But there was always the possibility that I wasn't, and if that was the case, I'd be better off knowing."

"Of course."

"When the result came back positive, I felt like I'd received a death sentence. It was a hundred times worse than what happened that night. I was depressed for months. Decided not to tell anyone. At times it felt like I was going to burst."

"That must have been incredibly difficult for you."

"It was," Brian acknowledged. "I did call a hotline a few times. They were good, talked me off the ledge. Not literally, I mean. I wasn't that low, but it was close sometimes."

"You've been through a lot."

"I wasn't feeling good about much," he concurred, "And then, out of the blue, I met Joe."

"He seems to bring you a lot of happiness."

"Yes, he does."

"What do you think about the idea of sharing with Joe what you've shared with me?"

"I've been thinking about it a lot," he said pensively. "I feel it's time."

"Are you sure?"

"I'm scared that he'll reject me... but if there's no real honesty, and you can't share your life experiences and deepest fears with your partner, then there's not much basis for a true relationship, is there?"

"Good point. Do you think you're ready for the consequences of your disclosure?"

"I am," Brian replied, recalling the thought he had that first day waiting outside of Rafael's office.

I owe it to Joe to at least try.

Once outside the office, Brian dialed Joe's number.

"Hey, Brian. Are you coming out of your squash game?"

"Joe, I haven't been going to squash every week."

"No?"

"I've been seeing a therapist."

"Oh? Okay. That's okay," Joe was surprised, but wanted to reassure him.

"I know we didn't make arrangements, but can I see you later tonight?"

"Sure," Joe replied. "Do you want to come around seven?"

"Yeah, that would be great."

"Is everything okay?"

"I need to talk with you about something important."

A rush of anxiety flooded Joe.

"Do you want to end our relationship?"

"No, silly." Brian smiled at the irony. "Quite the opposite."

62

"That's a relief." Joe laughed nervously. "Then I'll be all ears."

James

Briefcase in hand, James kissed his wife Inga on the cheek as he left for work at the software company. Stepping out of his apartment building in Tribeca, he merged into the crowd, an ant among ants, weaving toward Franklin Street subway station. Inga would leave in another hour, heading to the flower shop she owned on a nearby street corner.

Him in the office, her in the store.

James liked to be tidy and predictable. He believed there was a certain way of doing pretty much everything and once something was begun, it should be seen through to the end. How a shirt is starched and pressed, how a toilet is cleaned, how vegetables and meat are arranged on a plate. He shared all of these beliefs with Inga, who duly noted them and complied. She found it easier to keep the peace that way. It wasn't as if he abused her. What he asked her to do, he also did himself. They had been married for over two decades, with a couple of boys, now young men, attending college in California and Colorado.

He found "rape" too harsh a word. Even thinking it made him wince. James preferred to envision himself playing with someone until they were overpowered. This is what gave him the biggest thrill, feeling the person was there only for his pleasure. Owning them.

James's tastes had evolved over time. He loved Inga and the boys. Perfect wife, kids, apartment, job. Several colleagues were envious; he seemed to have it all. But, to James, it was all following a conventional plan, fulfilling expectations set by others. Something was missing.

Over the last few years Inga had lost interest in sex. It wasn't noticeable at first. It came to James one day, as he sat in his office, that he couldn't recall the last time his wife

64

initiated an act of intimacy. While Inga didn't refuse his advances, she too, appeared to be going through the motions. Making love, it seemed to James, was another run-of-the-mill household chore like sorting the laundry basket or washing plates after dinner. This made James somewhat angry and moderately depressed. After all, he still had desires and a healthy sex drive.

He began to find thrills online, in the form of chatrooms. It began by enjoying flirting with women, many of them married, yet craving sex with another man. Soon after, James dared himself to make the shift from fantasy to reality. To his surprise, women found his nondescript looks, glasses, and general bookishness to be strangely appealing. His sexual appetite was satisfied through equally hungry women, similarly bored. Happy to provide them with a no-strings encounter in their home or a hotel, James found great enjoyment in these secretive unions. And while the intrigue gave him a reason to roll out of bed in the morning, the bed from which he rolled was always his own. An overnighter would be crossing the line. Besides, he liked to hear Inga snooze peacefully, close by, in the warmth of the bed where their children were conceived. Psychological compartmentalization came easy to James; it was as simple as choosing the right room to put your thoughts in and then lock the door.

What began as a tentative exploration of curiosity had slipped into a compulsion that, in turn, soon grew into a full-fledged addiction. Daring himself to enter more and more chatrooms, James discovered their variability, each dedicated to specific fantasies and practices: cuckolding threesomes, sadomasochistic pet play, interracial sex, foot fetishes, bare-backing, breath-hoods...the options seemed endless. More intriguing, he found, were personal ads reflecting all kinds of people's desires in various combinations. There were sections for Men Looking for Women, Women Looking for Women, Women Looking for Men, Men Looking for Men, Anything Goes, and Brief Encounters. Examining ads in every section,

65

James was fascinated by their specificity, ranging from innocuous contents of some to the deeply disturbing nature of others. What united them, he noticed, was openly admitting secret desires in public to pursue others with similar tastes. Each ad was a planet moving in a vast universe of inexplicable needs, hoping to collide with another. "For every S, there's an M," he thought.

After randomly browsing through several sections one day, James casually opened the Men Looking for Men link. There were requests for anonymous trysts in hotel rooms and parks, but his attention was caught by a personal ad that read:

> The door will be unlocked. Enter quietly. I'll be sleeping face down on the bed. Do what you have to do. Don't wake me up. Then leave. No talking needed. No questions. Me: Good-looking, 32 years old, originally from Poland, gymnast body. You: Body type, race, age unimportant.

James kept reading it over and over again, imagining the soft creak of the door, semi-darkness inside, giving way to a dim nightlight from within the bedroom, guiding him like a beacon to his desire. He couldn't get the image out of his mind, logging on to view it a second day. Then a third. On the fourth, he responded and was summarily provided with a downtown address and set time.

The scene was just as described. Not even a whimper from the man, exciting James even more.

To his surprise and delight, the sleeping scenario was popular among pleasure seekers. There were variations involving requests for handcuffs, leather gloves, and complete darkness. In these encounters James discovered men's bodies, finding them strange at first, firmer flesh and hairier skin. To his delight, they were also more pliant and willing. However, none had lived up to the same intensity of his first experience. Breaking his own rule, James returned to the first man.

They enjoyed their time together so much, it became habitual.

The very promise of their meeting got James through each week. Staring through the office window, he'd indulge in flashbacks where he tweaked a certain move or changed positions. Given the frequency of their arrangement, it was only a matter of time before the fourth wall of their staged fantasy would break. One day, the man initiated a conversation. James found his voice surprisingly sweet. His name was Marcus and he wanted to take the game up a notch.

"What do you mean?" asked James.

"Well, you know how I'm tired, and I deliberately don't move?"

"Yes?"

"It's because I take a mild sedative. Nothing really strong, usually a couple of Valium or Xanax."

"What are you actually saying?" probed James. "What do you want to change?"

"I want to take some heavier sedatives," Marcus said. "Instead of being semi-comatose when you arrive, I want to be actually asleep. In a deep sleep," adding, "When I wake up there'll be no evidence of you ever having been here."

"Sure. Why not?"

They agreed, each gaining more satisfaction in a way neither could explain.

"I want to take it up another notch," Marcus said sometime later.

"How so?"

"Meet me in a bar, just like strangers do, and put a sedative in my drink. Then, when I'm helpless, bring me home and put me to bed. Whatever else you do, is up to you."

The idea excited James. Except for one aspect.

"I don't go into those bars."

"They're no different than the other bars," countered Marcus. "No one will recognize you. If it makes you feel better, wear a baseball cap and sunglasses."

It was James' first time inside a gay bar and, just as Marcus said, it was the same as any other. Except, perhaps, for the posters of impossibly muscled men more akin to superheroes than mere mortals. Pulling up a seat at the bar next to Marcus, James said "hello" before easing into a mundane exchange of pleasantries. They agreed that the sedative would be light just in case anything went wrong with the new scenario. There was always the option of more at home, later. When Marcus confessed to feeling tired, it appeared more like he was drunk. James then volunteered to take him home, telling the bartender he was a friend and knew where Marcus lived. In turn, he received a knowing *good luck* wink.

"See you guys next time," the bartender called after them, picking up his tip.

They did return, willingly, like a rinse and repeat cycle of dirty laundry. James liked predictability, a guarantee of knowing what he'd experience. He loved being in another world. What James had with Marcus felt distinct, very much separate from his "real" life. So much so, it had developed into a force unto itself, the most fulfilling part of his existence. A relationship once based purely on mutual fantasy had grown into a form of mutual dependency. James couldn't imagine his week without Marcus and vice versa. Like clockwork, they'd meet at the same time in different bars, strike up brief and idle chit chat, share a taxi ride to Marcus's home, all in anticipation of the impending scenario that originally brought them together.

Occasionally, James wondered what the origin was—if there were one at all—of Marcus's fantasy, an act they both felt compelled to repeat. He sensed it served a purpose, providing a form of out-of-body-out-of-mind experience, so intense it made everything else fade away for Marcus during that short period of time. It struck him as an addiction.

Then one day it was over, as swift as a flick of a switch, conveyed in an email.

James,

Don't come to the bar tomorrow. By the time you read this I will have left town. Something has happened that I can't explain right now. I won't be coming back. I'm sorry that this is abrupt, but it's better this way. I'll never forget you.

Marcus

James re-read the message several times, without any sign of emotion. But inside, Marcus's cryptic, sudden goodbye plunged James into freefall. He felt himself tumbling in slow motion through a tall glass building, each floor shattering into a thousand pieces, bursting like fireworks, one after another. Everything he'd carefully guarded for years was falling apart.

As originally planned, James went to the bar they'd agreed upon that night. It was new to him, a big place with different types of rooms. A large crowd surrounded a pianist who thumped the keys with aplomb as customers all joined into a chorus of *Somewhere* from West Side Story. Too loud. Catching a glimpse of the bar in the adjacent room, James noticed it was less hectic, and made his way there.

"Is this seat taken?" he asked a 30-ish guy sitting on the adjacent stool.

"No, help yourself."

James' attention turned to the TV where Dolly Parton mouthed the words to *Jolene*, encouraging the crowd to join in. He wondered why the volume wasn't audible, unaware the concert was on a loop, sparing bartenders from hearing the same songs all night long. Unable to take their eyes off Dolly, both, he and the man sitting next to him, simultaneously reached for the basket of potato chips on the bar, fingers accidentally brushing. Recognizing they'd done the same thing, they laughed, and grabbed a handful. James took the opportunity to get a good look.

Hmmm. Quite a handsome face, nice body... Go for it.

"Do these taste a little stale to you?" He asked in a friendly tone, wrinkling his face.

"Kind of. But I'm feeling a bit hungry."

"My name's Marcus, by the way," said James.

"I'm Brian." He reached again to scoop another handful.

James noticed a shy smile, and an almost empty glass, before asking:

"Can I buy you a drink?"

"Sure," said Brian. "I guess there's no harm in that."

Inga

As an only child, now without parents, Inga sensed mortality leaning in close. She could feel its hot breath, panting slowly like an invisible animal, waiting patiently to pounce. Sooner or later, it would be her turn. Middle-age had brought certain assurances of having done things right (*the boys are up and out of the house*), having achieved a degree of security (*the flower store was a wise investment*), and a level of physical comfort (*our loft apartment is a lovely home*). Still, as she lay awake at night, Inga constantly wrestled with the dilemma of whether or not her life was well-lived?

The news had reached Inga via a phone call from her cousin Askel in Copenhagen. Although her father had been in ill health for some time, it was still a shock to Inga's system. Mercifully, it happened while he was sleeping through the night. This detail provided a small island of consolation amidst the sea of guilt currently engulfing her. Inga hadn't seen him for several years; the role of surrogate daughter taken on by Askel some time ago. Knowing he was provided care by a loving niece made Inga happy, although she knew he'd preferred it were his own child.

"At least he was in his own bed, in his own house," comforted her husband James. "Not in some old people's end-of-the-road home, reeking of urine." He had a point. "Remember when we visited my mother in that godawful place? Didn't you take a bottle of Chanel to spray the hallways?

Inga and James travelled to Denmark for the funeral. Askel had organized a simple service, with a few old friends and neighbors, and even fewer family members. As the boys never really had much contact with their grandfather and were now up to their necks in mid-semester exams, Inga thought it best they stay put. As for the store, she'd left it in the capable hands of her assistant manager, Tara, who she'd grown to trust with her confidences more than James. The day after the funeral, he'd returned to the U.S. for work. Tara noticed James had been uncharacteristically tense lately, working long hours. Meanwhile, Inga decided to stay in Copenhagen and do the required paperwork, as well as clear the house in preparation for sale, unsure of when she'd return.

Sitting alone in her parent's attic, surrounded by dusty belongings outliving their use years ago, Inga scanned the room. A sewing machine with missing parts; an abandoned electric keyboard; a shopping trolley with a broken wheel. Boxes piled upon boxes, old rugs rolled and stacked against rickety drawers. She accidentally knocked over a container of vinyl records, spilling its contents onto the floor. Elvis Presley looked up at Inga, a curved strand of black hair cleaving his forehead like a big comma.

Why hadn't he gotten rid of this stuff? Where do I even begin? It's going to take days.

But she was determined. After encouraging Askel to take whatever she wanted, Inga systematically went through the whole mess, determining which items went to charity and which to the garbage skip. During this tedious process, Inga discovered a plastic toolbox tucked under a pile of old towels. Curiosity piqued, she picked up the box. It wasn't heavy. Shaking it gently, she felt the contents hit the sides. It was locked.

Whatever's in there was intended to be private.

With no sign of a key, Inga pulled and pushed, before dropping the box to the floor in the far-fetched hope it would burst open. It was then she noticed a small degree of wiggle room between the lock and the box's lower section. Straining to look through this sliver of space, Inga discerned folded papers, densely packed together.

Intriguing.

Finding no bolt cutters in the house, she went next door to borrow a pair from Marete, a longtime neighbor who knew Inga since she was a girl.

"Yes, we have some. Let me look," said Merete, before changing tone and topic. "I'm sure it's hard for you to go through his things. Your dad was a nice man, a good neighbor. Kept to himself, especially since your mother died."

An awkward pause.

"Can I get you a tea or something?" Merete offered. "Would you like to eat with us tonight? Frederik would love to see you, I'm sure."

"Thank you," Inga said, touched by the invitation, yet feeling pressured to clear up her father's possessions. "But there's so much to do."

"You've come all the way to Copenhagen from New York," Merete gently scolded, "The least you can do is let me feed you some home cooking. Nothing fancy, just *frikadeller*. I suppose you call them meatballs now."

Hearing her mother's voice emerge to whisper a reminder about good manners, Inga reneged. "Of course, I'll be happy to come."

"Wonderful! Now let me see if I can find those things."

As Merete looked in the shed for bolt cutters, Inga remained in the living room, picturing her whispering mother—had she lived—looking something like her neighbor. Lean and tall, her long gray hair pulled back into an orderly bun. A kind, smiling face, with sparkling blue eyes framed by finely etched lines, barely discernable.

"Here they are!" Marete returned, holding them in the air.

"Thank you. I'll bring them back when I come for dinner."

There were letters, dozens of them in bundles, tied with string.

Inga eased the first one out of its binding and pulled a page from the envelope. She recognized her father's handwriting.

> *Dear Frida,*
> *It has been a month since we first met. I cannot get out of bed in the morning without thinking about you. I cannot go to work without thinking about you. I cannot go through the day without thinking about you. I cannot go to sleep without thinking about you...*

She put it down for a moment, looking into the box, noticing envelopes of a different shape and color, tied with the same string. Gently, she eased a letter out from that bundle. It was her mother's hand.

> *My Dearest Hans*
> *Last night when you took my hand, and we walked through the park, I was hoping that you'd kiss me again, like the first time. When you did, I felt something I've never felt before...*

Inga raised her eyes, feeling them fill with tears. Each of her hands held a love letter from her mother and father. They filled the toolbox.

They're private. Not meant for me... but I want to read their words.

74

She hesitated, searching for justification.

Aren't I a part of them, a result of their love? Now that they're gone, would they really mind?

Sitting cross-legged on the attic's bare floorboards, Inga pondered her dilemma. A decision had to be made. After a short period of reflection, she chose.

I'm going to do it. I want to know more about their lives, their world before me.

It was the late 1950s. Frida was training to be a secretary. Hans was working as a bus conductor, one of the youngest in service, collecting money and issuing tickets. She got on his bus one day at Tivoli Gardens, close to her office. He immediately noticed Frida's glacier-blue eyes framed by dark gold waves of hair reaching her shoulders. Trying not to be too obvious, Hans sneaked a peek. Frida, in turn, discretely took note of the handsome conductor who seemed quite young for such a job. His shift coincided with her journey home to her parents' house, and they began by casually saying hello. In those brief moments, Hans noticed a wide smile, projecting confidence. Conversely, Frida observed his shyer, more reserved smile, and green, hazel-flecked eyes.

After two weeks of sideways glances and small pleasantries, they ventured into conversation.

"Do you like to dance?" Hans asked Frida.

"I love to dance."

"Have you heard of a Hop?"

"Yes. I've never been to one but have always wanted to go."

Hops were new and exciting places, an idea imported from

75

America where teenagers danced to rock and roll, music quite different from their parents' generation.

"Friday night, then? I can pick you up at seven."

Frida and Hans both enjoyed themselves that night and made plans for a second date. Soon they began going for walks, chatting over a warm cup of coffee or a cold glass of beer, while exploring the city together.

They became intimate. It was the first time for both. Their initial awkwardness soon gave way to the discoveries of mutual sexual pleasure. The young lovers sought hidden places in darkened parks and the deep woods at the edge of the city. They also plotted strategic times to be alone when parents were out of the house shopping or visiting relatives. The world they shared enveloped them like a glorious bubble. Not much else mattered except being together.

Then Frida became pregnant; they were both nineteen. At first, she'd cried and cried, fearing the shame she'd bring to her parents. But Hans assured her it'd all be fine. They'd be getting married anyway, right? This would just speed things up a little. Once they shared the news with their families, and their four parents had time to react, they all came together to discuss the arrangements. All agreed a wedding was immanent, and the newlyweds were to live with Frida's parents.

On the big day, Hans thought his bride looked stunning in her embroidered white gown. Almost four months along, and undetectable to those who didn't know - Frida beamed radiantly. For those who did know, they took satisfaction in the fact that the right thing was being done. The baby would be "legitimate." As the time neared, and Frida grew large, both families excitedly prepared for their new member. A crib was bought, clothes knitted, blankets crocheted. All was in place and now, they waited.

76

When Frida entered the hospital, the intensity of the pain frightened her but the nurses said it was normal, and to keep calm.

The baby was a boy.

Stillborn. No one had expected this, least of all Frida and Hans.

Unable to move from the hospital bed, she cried for days until her face was red and puffy, her eyes, slits. Hans took time off work and sat beside Frida. Outwardly stoic, he looked on with concern, but inside, he felt hollow.

In turn, Frida and Hans comforted one another, for each could see the depth of the other's suffering, the feelings of responsibility for what had transpired. Against their parents' wishes, they decided to move to a small apartment where they could be alone with each other and help each other work through the pain, before planning a future together.

All of this Inga pieced together from arranging the dates of letters exchanged. The majority were written during their courtship, trailing off after the wedding, and beginning again when their baby died, lasting through Frida's long stay at the hospital. After that, they'd abruptly ended.

Inga hadn't known about the baby, she wished she'd been told. She could hear her mother's voice again, asking: *What would've been the point, my sweet? To share my pain? Isn't there enough in the world already? You'll have plenty of your own, my sweet. I wish it weren't so, but believe me, plenty.*

Inga had often thought it strange she'd been born sixteen years after her parents' marriage. "You were the one we'd always dreamed about," her father used to tell her. "We waited half our lives."

77

What was going through my mother's head for all of those years? Was she frightened to have another baby? What was it like for her to carry me and give birth? Did she fear I'd be dead, too?

Placing the letters back into their envelopes, Inga scooped them up into her arms like a baby and carried them to her bedroom. She'd slept all of her life in this room until leaving Denmark at age eighteen for the United States on a university scholarship. There, she'd met her future husband, James, studying alone one night in a computer lab on campus. To Inga's surprise, after the wedding she didn't wish to return to Denmark. Instead, they had settled down close to James' family. Before long, the kids were born, and then her florist business grew. As the years passed, and the busier she became, Inga visited her parents less and less. After her mother died, she barely went to Copenhagen.

Lying down on the bed, Inga looked at the ceiling as she had done thousands of times before. The same cracks were there, meandering like rivers on a map of a flat, unnamed country.

The act of closing her eyes made time melt away. Inga was seventeen years old now, imagining what lay ahead. She wanted to have a life well-lived. To be far, far away from dreary Denmark with its long winter nights and short, cool summers. She also desired to be far, far away from the prospect of a predictable marriage, like her parents', flattened into the cream-colored wallpaper of everydayness.

Now, she wondered about everything. Did her sons think the same way about her and James? They attended colleges on the other side of the country, as far away as they could get.

I can understand that. I did something similar.

Still, she felt bad.

I'll call them both later today. Ask how they are. Tell them I love them. How proud I am. Is it possible they have steady girlfriends there already? ... I never thought of it before, but the boys might actually settle where they are. Bring up their children there. Will that mean I won't see my grandchildren much?

James, too, had become distant. Lost interest. Didn't even put his arm around her in bed anymore. Said he had back pain and could only sleep on one side, facing away from her. Inga couldn't help but think it was a ruse for something she didn't know and couldn't understand.

The indignities we bear in our attempts to maintain a relationship.

She'd been good at going along with whatever James wanted, to maintain the peace, keep him happy. But was it worth maintaining? This was the question that had risen to the surface of her thoughts, as Inga lay awake each night. She'd begun to admit it wasn't. For some time now, Inga had been unable to accept the answer, the enormity of it all.

With her head comfortably on the pillow, Inga felt a sudden desire to shrink to the size of a microscopic insect, fly up, and crawl into a crack of the ceiling she'd always known. To leave everything behind and simply disappear into a safe, hidden place. In that instant, she felt utterly alone in the world, terrified of all that she did not know and may never understand.

Tara

"Hello, *Flower Power*. Tara speaking. How may I help you?"

"Do you have calla lilies?"

"Yes."

"In what colors?"

"We have them in white, yellow, and violet."

"They'll do."

Tara instantly made a mental calculation of the cost, added tax, and then a delivery charge. From the very start Inga, the store's owner, loved how quick she was with numbers.

She missed Inga. They had a long, good working relationship that had blurred into a personal one, through a sharing of mutual confidences. Tara was itching to marry her boyfriend, Malik. Inga kept reassuring her he'd likely pop the question soon. In turn, she shared worries about her husband working long hours. Tara suspected he might have someone; if he did, knowing James, he'd go about it quietly. Although she felt Inga deserved better, Tara kept her thoughts to herself. After all, she was still her boss.

Overseeing the store had been more work for Tara, but she'd done it before, always enjoying the challenge of running a business from soup to nuts. This meant buying boxes of flowers wholesale at the crack of dawn, creating displays, serving walk-in customers; responding to telephone requests, coordinating deliveries, balancing the books, and safely locking up at night. Inga paid generously for Tara's increased responsibilities, and she told herself the extra money would eventually come in handy, like for a wedding.

Her best friend Gloria stopped by the store whenever she had the chance.

"Aren't these calla lilies beautiful?" Tara asked.

"You know what they represent, right?"

"Weddings?"

"Girl, you have a one-track mind. It's death, they represent death."

"I knew that. Just teasing. Still, it doesn't change that they're my favorites. I'm not afraid of thinking about death."

"Speaking of which..." Gloria began, "I've been wanting to ask you something for a while."

"What is it?"

"I want to go see a Regression Therapist."

"What's that?"

"Someone who takes you back into your past lives."

"Like reincarnation?"

"Exactly. I've been wanting to do it forever but haven't had the guts." Gloria paused. "I don't suppose you'd be interested in going with me?"

Tara put her head to one side, as was her habit when weighing a decision.

"You wouldn't need to do anything, just sit with me," Gloria continued. "I've heard from a woman at my spiritualist group about a Dr. Petrossian who's talented in this area. Will you think about it?"

"Sure, I'll go," said Tara, always ready to support a friend.

"He's a quack!" Malik kept telling her, appalled at the tales Tara shared and the money Gloria spent.

"He's certified."

"In what field? Fraud?"

"There's a whole other world, Malik, be open to it. Who's to say it's any less worthy of the other things people believe in."

"Like what? Flying saucers?"

"No, silly. Religions. Spiritual things. Déjà vu. There's a lot we don't know about..."

"All I'm saying...be careful. Or you'll be sucked in and become addicted."

"I haven't even tried yet."

Tara rolled her eyes, signaling an unspoken but clearly communicated *puh-lease*. She considered her budding fascination with past life regression something to be explored, like taking a graduate class at the New School, only more interesting.

"And...this Dr. Whosehisface is addicted to money," Malik continued. "Regression *therapist,*" he mocked. "*Certified...* maybe by his cousin higher up in their pyramid scheme."

"Don't knock what you haven't tried," Tara shot back.

He sighed and shook his head.

"Don't say I didn't warn you."

Dr. Petrossian's apartment was in an old, French-inspired building on East 66th Street between Park and Madison. Tara noticed the high ceilings, gilded cornices, and purple velvet curtains blocking light from the outside world. Everything exuded faded grandeur, a sense of time standing still, including the doctor himself. They'd been ushered into a special regression room and directed to sit on an antique chaise lounge with crimson upholstery and ornate carvings. On a nearby table was a dimly lit Tiffany lamp, ringed with designs of violet dragonflies on emerald lily pads. Opposite the chaise lounge was an elevated, throne-like seat in which Dr. Petrossian sat while conducting business.

"When I count to three and snap my fingers, you'll be where you need to be," he instructed Gloria. "Are you ready?"

"Ready," she said with a hint of trepidation as she closed her eyes.

"If you're sitting comfortably, then I'll begin." Dr. Petrossian cleared his throat One. Two. Three." He snapped his fingers with a flourish. "Tell me what you see, what you feel...?"

Sitting next to her on the couch, Tara saw Gloria's eyes begin to dilate beneath their lids as she began to gently sway back and forth...

"There's a park. People in it..."

"What are they wearing? Describe them."

Gloria shared that she had been Henry in a former life, a pale, scrawny, petty thief in nineteenth-century England before being caught stealing a leg of lamb and shipped for life to a Tasmanian penal colony. There, he died, three years later,

83

from tuberculosis and was buried in an unmarked grave by other unhealthy convicts who'd soon follow in his steps.

"Are you feeling alright, Henry?" asked Dr. Petrossian.

She'd stopped swaying. Gloria hunched over, her arms crossed and her hands vigorously rubbed her shoulders.

"I'm cold."

"It's fine, don't worry. When I count backwards from three, you'll be leaving a chilly place and transitioning to your current incarnation. And...Three. Two. One." He clicked his fingers.

Gloria opened her eyes and was back.

"Now," he turned to Tara. "Are you ready to try?"

A doorway had opened, beckoning with an invisible hand. The doctor's voice was too seductive to resist.

"Ready."

"If you're sitting comfortably, I'll begin, Tara. One. Two. Three." He snapped his fingers. "What do you see?"

"There's a big white house, surrounded by trees, and fields stretching into the distance..."

"Who else is there?"

"People in the fields. It's hot. Some are stripped to the waist."

"Describe them."

"Black. They're all dark-skinned."

84

"And you?"

"Black, too. Standing at the edge of a field. Calling to the folks to come eat. Food is ready. Temperature so hot. Heat rising from the land." She paused, and in a southern drawl asked, "May I have some water, please?" touching her throat.

Gloria poured a glass of water from a nearby decanter, and Tara continued her story.

She was Matilda, age fifteen, a house slave; also daughter of the plantation's' master, a man who had habitually forced himself upon her mother. Lighter skinned than those in the fields, Matilda had been made to work in the big house. The mistress hated her, suspecting Matilda's origin, and aware of her purpose: the very same man who had violated her mother now visited Matilda some nights. Lying beneath him, bearing his mechanical movements accompanied by grunts and snorts, Matilda's eyes would fix upon the stars seen through the small window, and her spirit would fly toward them seeking refuge. Having little else to comfort her in life, she was grateful for their embrace.

"It's time to transition back," Tara heard Dr. Petrossian's voice. "And...Three. Two..."

She obeyed, feeling a warmth course throughout her body as she shifted into herself.

In the days that followed, Tara wasn't sure how she felt other than being profoundly touched to experience both Matilda's strength and sadness.

When she finally told Malik, he freaked out.

"That sounds awful! Aren't you traumatized? He could be damaging you with this stuff."

"I know it sounds strange, and the circumstances were horrible, but it was more like I was an actor in a film. It still was me...but I felt detached."

"You know how this works, right?"

"What do you mean?"

"Tara don't be so naïve. This is what happens. You get hypnotized by a shyster. He's going to tell you to recall memories of experiences you've never really had, but you think you have, because he's feeding you questions, and it seems so.... normal. But in answering him you're building your own picture. We all know about the past, carry impressions from seeing films, documentaries, books, learning stuff from an early age. Once these images come into your head, they *seem* real, and under hypnosis you can't tell them from what *is* real. It's a scam."

But it didn't seem that way to her.

"It's hard to explain fully." She needed to counter Malik's challenge. "It's more somatic - I just *feel* it. I actually feel what I see. And once I've done that, the whole thing makes sense."

It was Malik's turn to roll his eyes.

That neither of them could resist Dr. Petrossian's allure didn't matter to Tara and Gloria. Weekly visits to cross thresholds into former lives brought them even closer together. They agreed that people wouldn't understand and think only about the money.

"Each incarnation teaches lessons to be brought with you into your next life," he explained.

In addition to being a British convict shipped to Australia, Gloria had variously embodied: a Vietnamese soldier in the

American War, debilitated by Agent Orange; a nineteenth-century New Orleans Madame who parlayed her bordello into a sizable real estate fortune; a Polynesian artisan on Rapa Nui, creating jewelry from abalone shells; and a female warrior in the African kingdom of Dahomey, who slayed three Frenchmen in a ferocious battle at Cotonou.

"Damn, girl! You've lived," said Tara.

"You ain't done so bad yourself."

It was true. Tara had not only been Matilda, but also: a member of the Spanish Inquisition, torturing suspected heathens in Southern Spain; a fourteenth-century Chinese woman with highly prized lotus feet; a sought-after scribe who wore a prosthetic foot in ancient Egypt; and a Romanian circus acrobat who lost her grip and plummeted from the trapeze to a messy death in front of horrified children.

All of these incarnations intrigued Tara. Each time was like entering a mysterious world similar to Alice stepping through the looking glass into Wonderland.

Then, one time, it was different.

"Where are you?" asked Dr. Petrossian, sitting on this throne-like chair.

"On a bridge."

"What's your name?"

"Cornelia Davis."

"Cornelia, who else can you see?"

"A crowd. There's a crowd of angry people."

"Where are they?

"Not far from me."

"What are they doing?"

"Shouting."

"What are they shouting?"

"It's hard to hear. There are so many, and they're very loud. Angry."

"How are they dressed?"

"In plain clothes. Women in long, black skirts. Heads covered in white. Men with hats, wide brims, pants to the knee...long socks...big shoes."

"Cornelia, are you—"

"I can hear what they're shouting now..."

"What is it?"

"'Witch.' They're shouting 'witch,' over and over." Her breath became short. "They're putting a rope around my body. No! No! Stop! Stop!"

Cornelia began to struggle. Her hands flailed in the air around her, suddenly becoming rigid by her sides.

"Come back to us, Tara," instructed Dr. Petrossian.

"Tara, you're scaring me," said Gloria, "Get back here, now!"

The rope was hurting. It was too tight. Cornelia couldn't move. Her forearms were pressed to her sides and her hands were bound behind her back. People were shouting, "In the water! In the water!" staring with rabid eyes, pointing fingers loaded with hate. She felt faint and a violent urge to vomit.

"Help me!" she shouted, "Somebody help me."

Several men closed in, making Cornelia take a step backwards. She felt her spine push into the rough, wooden rail of the bridge.

"It's not too late," one of them said through gritted teeth. "Confess!"

"Do it! Do it! Do it!" The crowd chanted in unison.

Cornelia looked down at the fast-flowing water twenty feet below, and then at the chaplain next to her.

"If you're guilty, you'll survive. If you're innocent, you'll drown," adding, "May God Bless you!"

"No!" screamed Cornelia. "Stop! Stop!"

"We'll soon see," said a man next to the chaplain, face hardened by hate.

With a scoop of his thick forearm, she was horizontal on the rail of the bridge.

Cornelia was pushed by several pairs of hands. Facing the water from above. Feeling the rope tightly wound around her torso, she was falling in slow motion,

Air swept into her open mouth and over burning cheeks, pulling the hair away from her face as she strained with hands tied.

89

The water moving toward her, Cornelia glimpsed short-lived bursts of foam and noticed bubbles where the currents crossed.

She pierced the water with a single, loud splash.

Cold.

Silent screams.

The pull of a powerful undercurrent. Bursting lungs. Moving fast. Rope violently yanked taut, like a dropped anchor. Sudden, searing pain. Head breaking the surface. Sucking in air. Spitting out frigid water. Coils of swirling hair obscuring vision. Bobbing at the end of a rope - like a toy boat. Moving legs. Treading water. Head thrust back. Looking at the sky. Gasping. Concentrating on staying alive.

Focus.

Keep legs moving.

Silence from the crowd as they watch the struggle. Then heaviness. Weight of water. Slipping back under the surface. Swallowing. Rising to the light again. Spitting it out. Back under. More water. Darker, colder. Surface again. Weaker. Coughing.

Can't get it all out.

Sliding back under. Legs tired. Over and over.

Please, God.

The weight. Pulling now.

Please God.

Bringing her down.

Not like this.

Back to the surface, almost. Sky bleary through the water. So bright. For a moment. Then gray. Grayer. Down.

Please.

Down.

God.

Down.

"Tara! Tara!" She heard shouting from a distance, echoing through a long hallway.

Vaguely familiar voices.

"Tara! Come back! Come back!"

She opened her eyes and found two panic-stricken faces.

"Are you okay?" Gloria asked repeatedly.

It's important to stay with us now," Dr. Petrossian instructed. "Stay with us."

"I'm fine," Tara said. "Just a little tired. What happened?

"You don't know?" Gloria asked, somewhat bewildered.

"Know what?"

"All of that stuff you just told us."

"What stuff?"

"The people shouting. Thinking you're a witch. Throwing you off a bridge. Drowning?"

"Really? No, I —" Tara's expression changed as she felt a sudden pain.

"What is it?" Gloria was alarmed.

Tara placed her hands on her chest.

"What is it?"

"I—I can't breathe—" Tara managed to say, her face contorting.

"Doctor! Do something!"

"I'm not that kind of doctor," he said, fear in his voice.

"No matter—"

Intuitively, Tara pushed her hands down hard on her own chest, repeatedly. Her mouth opened.

Out of it sprayed the contents of her lunch, mixed with stomach juices, projected with great velocity, onto Gloria and Dr. Petrossian. They remained fixed in disbelief, like statues, as Tara convulsed, and the flow continued to douse their bodies with spasmodic, forceful spurts.

After several quick twitches the fetid liquid stopped as suddenly as it had begun.

Tara watched it drip steadily from their still faces.

No one could say a word.

Malik

You'd think vegans living in this city would have more options.

That's how it all started. Ruminations on the paucity of good eateries.

Malik played with the idea of opening a restaurant, knowing it would be a huge leap in terms of committing finances and time. On the upside, he'd benefit from channeling all of his energies into something productive. On the downside, it would be like putting all of his beans in one basket. Still, his girlfriend Tara was supportive of his ideas, offering to help in any way she could.

He couldn't believe his luck finding a modest-sized, affordable place on Sullivan Street, two blocks south of Washington Square Park; the area was a hive of activity, swarming with NYU students. At first sight it looked like the proverbial hole in the wall with a tiny kitchen, not big enough to swing a radish. Nonetheless, all Malik could see was possibilities. It could seat up to sixteen people, if the chairs were slim and portable.

Nothing ventured, nothing gained.

These were his thoughts when signing the lease. It was a good deal on a busy street where eateries were wedged between one another, with enough customers to go around.

On one side of him was budget-friendly *Mamoun's Shawramarama*, and on the other, the upmarket *Carmen's Veranda*, a Brazilian churrascaria serving steaks so big they hung off plates. *Mamoun's* catered to sneakers and flip-flop wearers, *Carmen's* to well-heeled clientele. Malik wanted his place to appeal to both and attract the noticeably absent Birkenstock and Croc crowd.

What would be the name of *his* restaurant? A hundred possibilities had gone through his head along with the shortcomings of each. He'd condensed the list, even sorting them into categories, and kept going back and forth on their merits. There were obvious ones such as *Going Green, Herbivore,* or *V is for Vegan.* Ones he considered a little edgier, and perhaps more memorable, included *The Vegan Vault, Like a Vegan,* and *Raw and Ready.* In the catchy-but-corny sub-list was *A New Leaf of Life, Root 66, Veganopolis, Veg Table,* and *Figs in a Blanket.* The silly-but-still-possible category incorporated *Smoothie Operator, Hail Kale!, Soy Joy, The Veggie Wedgie, Lovegetable,* and the three-pronged options of *Lettuce Eat, Lettuce Spray,* and *Lettuce Love.* Malik was driving himself bananas over this decision. As much as he liked some of these possibilities, he held a lingering desire to see his name on the awning.

Ultimately, he settled on *Malik's Vegan Bistro,* imagining the place as a romantic destination. Tables would have flickering candles above, and customers would have interlocking legs below. Lunch special from 12-3, dinner served 6-11, closed on Mondays. An excellent chef himself, all Malik needed was a prep chef, dishwasher, and a two-wait staff, who came in the shape of Nico, Peter, Lizzy, and Latisha.

That was a year ago. Since then, the place had gained a reputation for interesting food combinations and unusual dishes. Malik's beetroot burger with sesame dressing was featured in New York Magazine, and his blueberry and peach crisp sold out before it left the oven. All his employees had stayed with him and, true to her word, Tara pitched in on weekends and in the evenings when the place was busiest.

One Saturday when Lizzy had the night off, Tara helped carry and fetch plates. She noticed a customer sitting alone take off her hoodie and recognized a world-famous singer.

94

Wearing sweatpants, no make-up, and hair pulled back into a ponytail, the singer raised her Jackie-O sunglasses to look at the menu.

"Tara whispered to Latisha as she passed by holding two bowls of tahini lemon quinoa with asparagus ribbons. "Do you see who's over there? It's Majella."

Latisha squinted inconspicuously.

"Girl, are you sure that's her?"

"Mmm-hmm."

"I better take her order, then."

Latisha had seen, and served, some famous people in her time, but Majella was legendary, known around the world for her daring personality and innovative dance music.

As Latisha approached her table, Majella said:

"I'm waiting for someone."

"Can I get you something while you're waiting?"

"I'll have a lime juice with mint and ginger."

Tara alerted Malik who peered from the kitchen. He was already wondering if she'd take a photograph with him before leaving, to go with the framed ones he had up of Shia LaBeouf, Chelsea Clinton, and the Mayor. Restaurant owners knew which side their bread was buttered on. Celebrity photos put them on the map.

"I'd read she was a vegan," he said. "Has her own chef."

"Should I go over and say something?" asked Tara.

"Nahhh, let's just leave her be." He was already practicing what he'd say to her. "You know it's a New York City custom not to bother famous folks."

When Latisha returned with Majella's drink, two men on the adjacent table had begun a conversation with her.

"My name's Ravi," said the Indian man. "This is my partner, Tony. We've bought your albums for over twenty years. Absolutely love them. *Further and Further* is my favorite. Although," he caught himself, "Of course I love them all."

"*We* do," affirmed Tony nervously. "We do love them all."

Majella nodded, and said "Thank you, guys. Nice to meet you," before returning to the menu.

"Here's your drink," Latisha placed it on the table while flashing a look at Ravi and Tony that said *be cool, leave her be,* telepathically transmitting: *Don't ask her for an autograph.*

"Thanks," said Majella. "Oh, hi!" She raised her hand slightly as a man entered the restaurant. "I got here a little early," she said as he approached the table. They kissed each other on the cheek. "Menu looks great. Take a seat."

He was tall, the color of caramel, with prominent cheekbones, and shoulder-length black hair. Probably thirty years younger than her.

"Can I get you something to drink, sir?"

"That looks good." He signaled to Majella's glass. "One of those, please."

Latisha and Tara congregated in a small nook of the kitchen.

"Do you think he's a date?" Tara asked.

"Maybe."

"They say she likes them younger."

"Why shouldn't she? No one makes a fuss when guys are with women younger than their daughters."

"True. He *is* cute."

"You two quit gossiping," Malik admonished half joking, half serious. "There's work to be done. Just make sure she's happy. This could give us good publicity."

As it happened, Majella wasn't on a date. She was working—interviewing dancers for her next world tour. Now conducting round two, she spent a little one-on-one time with each candidate, to see if they were a good fit for her personality and, preferably, fun to be with. The dancer's name was Patricio.

"How bad do you want this job?" she asked.

"I'd sell my mother to get it."

"Now we're getting somewhere." She raised her glass.

Majella ordered squash broth with shredded legume for an appetizer, and Patricio, grilled artichokes with heart of palm and saffron aioli. From what Latisha could gather, as she eavesdropped on snatches of their conversation, the interview included a history of his dancing accomplishments, workout routines, ability to play well with others, and sexual preferences.

For their main courses, Majella—usually hyper-disciplined in terms of food—decided to indulge and order a grilled vegetable casserole. It would be the first time she'd eaten a sauce for half a year. Patricio went with the beetroot burger and parsnip fries.

After placing their dishes on the table, Latisha returned to the kitchen for two more drinks.

"Whatever they're talking about," she said to Tara, "she's laughing up a storm."

"This sauce is delicious," Majella said as she began to pick at her casserole. "I wonder what's in it?"

It was then she noticed a shape move across the wall next to her shoulder.

"Ugh," she leaned back in her chair. "A giant bug!"

There it was, the size and color of a large date, scuttling slowly with long antennae sweeping the wall, making it look even bigger.

"Do something!" she said, rearing away.

Quickly, Patricio reached over and swiped at the insect with the intention of swatting it onto the floor. He clipped it, causing the giant cockroach to plummet directly into Majella's casserole. Both looked down at the spectacle of a massive insect mired in thick, sludgy sauce.

"Motherfucker, do something!" she shouted, abandoning all pretense of a low-key presence.

Patricio seized Majella's spoon and began heaping more sauce over the giant cockroach, burying it mercilessly like a gangster's victim in cement. For a moment, the casserole looked calm. But before long, one spot in the sauce began to rise and fall, rise and fall, as the primordial strength of the insect drove on against the odds.

As they both stared in disbelief, the insect appeared to recover from the trauma of premature burial in the form of a miniature beating heart. Unsteadily, but with recognizable strength, a leg poked through the sauce. Majella and Patricio looked on, even more horrified, unsure if the circular movements were the first step of an escape attempt or simply a flailing limb in the throes of an unlikely death-by-vegan-haute-cuisine.

Feeling it needed finishing off, Patricio shoveled on more sauce.

Within a few seconds, Majella donned her hoodie, put on sunglasses, and slipped out the front door leaving him, spoon in hand. He sat there, not quite sure of what just happened.

Tara noticed the commotion and alerted Malik that something was occurring at their table. By the time Malik walked over, all he saw was a man holding a spoon repeatedly muttering, "Shit. I didn't get the job!"

"Is everything okay?" Malik asked, even though he could see otherwise.

"There's a goddam giant cockroach in the food."

"Impossible," Malik stated. "I prepared it myself."

At the adjacent table, Ravi had watched everything from the corner of his eye. Leaning over he asked, "Didn't you knock it in when you tried to kill it?"

Patricio stood up and shouted, "Fuck this place! It has giant cockroaches and I've just lost a fucking dream job," before walking out.

Malik expected the customers to rise up and leave, filled with disgust. Instead, they sat still.

If this gets out, it could be the end of my restaurant.

"It's not your fault," said Tony, "I saw it too. The guy knocked it in there."

"Don't worry," another customer said. "This is New York for God's sake. Those things get everywhere. There was one in my bathroom last week, and I'm a clean freak."

"We've been here several times," reassured another woman, "Everything's always good."

Somewhat calmed, Malik removed the casserole from the vacated table.

"This is going into the toilet," he said to Tara and Latisha.

"These things can stand a nuclear blast. We don't want it reappearing like The Creature from the Black Lagoon."

"What if it gets out?" asked Tara.

"It can't if I flush."

"No, not that. The story," she clarified.

"Let's hope it doesn't."

The following Monday, when Latisha arrived at work, she plopped The New York Post on the table.

"Did you read Page Six?"

Page Six always featured a section by an influential gossip columnist who delighted in spilling the beans about celebrity sightings, especially those caught in compromising situations. Names and places were bolded for readers to zoom in to select the tasty morsels they wished to consume. Occasionally, there'd be a box for a highlighted story.

"Look at the box," she directed.

His eyes located it and Malik began to read.

Did it Jump or was it Pushed?

Reliable sources inform us that **Majella** was dining on the down-low in **Malik's Vegan Bistro** on Sullivan Street with a new, as yet unnamed, suitor. Dressed for disguise in big shades and a hooded sweatshirt, a million miles from her glamorous videos, Majella and her alleged new boy toy had a public spat. Matters erupted when a giant cockroach landed in her meal causing Majella to be in a bigger spin than her early records. A question arose as to whether her aspiring knight in shining armor tried to remove it from a wall and in doing so made matters so much worse. The incident obviously bugged her as she was seen leaving without her young suitor. Oh, to have been a fly—definitely not a bug—on the wall for *that* conversation.

Malik put his head in hands.

Fuck! That's it. No more restaurant. My dream's down the drain.

"This is a thousand times worse than I thought."

"Are you kidding?" Latisha laughed. "There's no such thing as bad publicity. You're on page six of The Post."

"I've a feeling this may be an exception to that rule."

"I don't. This could be the beginning of Vegan World." Optimism infused Latisha's voice. "The spark to launch a franchise of beet burgers, from sea to shining sea."

The telephone rang.

"Malik's Vegan Bistro. How can I help you?"

"Office of Health Inspection," a woman said in an official tone. "We need to schedule a visit."

His heart sank fast, like a stone in water.

I was right. Everything will be lost.

"Just kidding," the voice changed into Tara's. "Had you for a moment there."

Latisha

I could have done better than that. Much better.

Sitting in the darkened theater, squashed into a century-old seat recently refurbished in plush red velvet, Latisha watched the play with passionate indifference. She focused like a laser beam on the actress playing the character of Madeline, the female protagonist's younger sister. Brash, bold, outspoken, larger than life—everything Latisha had ever wanted to have in a role.

I almost got that part.

At least that's what Latisha told herself. She'd answered the cattle call, been to an initial audition, and done good enough reading to receive a call back. In the second round she, along with fourteen other hopefuls, now performed in costume. Pink halter-neck. Big flares. Hoop earrings the size of dinner plates so heavy they made her lobes sag.

I can do it. I can do it.

Good Times, Bad Rhymes was an offbeat love story that took place in the mid-70s, set in a nightclub of excessive drink and drugs. The vulnerable-but-street savvy heroine was pursued by an endless stream of scheming men. A TV star eager to prove herself on the boards had already secured the role; it was the younger sister, Madeline, that Latisha firmly set her sights on.

She had to perform a couple of short scenes and deliver a brief monologue. Having studied the script endlessly for days, Latisha knew it inside and out. She even called in sick to her waitressing job. Thankfully, her boss's girlfriend, Tara, was available, and could fill in for Latisha.

She left the audition thinking, *Nailed it.*

103

Please, God. Pretty please. This could be my break.

Opening her email, the following day, she read:

Dear Latisha Jefferson,

We regret to share with you that you were not selected for the part of Madeline in *Good Times, Bad Rhymes*. Competition was exceptionally high due to a very talented pool of applicants. That you made it to the second round means that the casting director and her assistants definitely recognized your talent. We wish you good luck in all of your future endeavors.

Robert Del Valle,

Casting Director

Leaving the theater, Latisha couldn't pick her head up: she felt the weight of the world on her shoulders. She looked at marks made by discarded gum, flattened by thousands of feet, reminding her of little clouds in the dark gray sky of the sidewalk. Heading home on the subway to Harlem, she kept saying to herself:

I could've done that. When will it be my turn?

Over ten years ago Latisha had moved to New York from Allentown, Pennsylvania, looking for a break in the entertainment world. She'd been close a few times. The closest, perhaps, an advertisement for a fungal nail treatment by a company seeking to expand their demographic to a younger audience. While a foot in the door, she didn't enjoy being recognized in public as the girl with green toenails. Small roles in smaller productions occasionally came her way, ranging from a giant chinchilla to a psychopathic nun wielding a chainsaw at a teenage beach party. Hardly Lady Macbeth or Hedda Gabbler. Still, Latisha persevered, telling herself she was learning the trade, and everyone who made it started somewhere.

Her parents, initially supportive of Latisha's choices in her early 20s, were now less inhibited to make suggestions about Plan B or C, or even D. Perhaps teaching elementary school? Nurse's aide? Office temp?

Lately, Latisha had been feeling down. Life in general hadn't been coming together in the way she'd imagined. Waiting tables had always struck her as a rite of passage for New York actors, serving as a means to an end, quick money to cover rent, pay for acting classes, and keep an agent. Latisha loved the buzz of talking to fellow hopeful artists who treaded water by bartending, selling clothes, and waitressing. Their natural camaraderie helped maintain them as they worked toward their dreams. Everyone in her circle introduced themselves first as a singer, musician, actor, dancer, writer. After a few drinks, it would come out that they were "picking up some hours" selling shoes, serving ice cream, or mixing cocktails. Such was the manifestation of hope.

How long can I keep telling myself this story?

Will it ever be my turn?

She'd also fallen in love and it pained her deeply that it was one-sided.

Malik. Her boss.

It had started some time ago, when her friend Akemi, another aspiring actress, told her of a restaurant in the Village that was about to open - she had seen a Help Wanted sign in the window. Timing was good. Latisha was tired of long shifts in her current gig, a midtown steakhouse geared to please tourists. Latisha and Malik instantly made favorable impressions on one another.

Malik was a hard worker, he wanted to bring veganism up a notch, and challenge the public's impression of bland food unable please taste buds or fill a stomach to satisfaction. Latisha saw how hard he worked to developed new dishes that looked good and tasted better. She was wowed by his pumpkin risotto and crispy mushrooms, in awe of his okra jambalaya. What sealed the deal was Malik's rasta pasta, made with slivers of red, yellow, and green peppers. Latisha recognized that not only was he amazing in the kitchen, but he was also an all-round nice guy too, treating all employees the same as customers, with kindness and respect.

Latisha confided to Akemi her secret love of Malik.

"Be careful," Akemi counselled. "I don't want to see you get hurt."

Although Latisha had been around this block a few times before, it didn't make it any easier. In fact, it made it a little harder. Viewing herself as a realist, rather than a home wrecker, she knew what the outcome would likely be. In order to survive, however, she reframed her situation to being one of a friendship for which she was grateful. After all, it was a rare thing for a boss to treat her as an equal.

Malik, for his part, liked Latisha, as did his girlfriend, Tara. The size of the restaurant meant everyone worked closely together, both physically in terms of tight space, and psychologically, as everyone involved wanted Malik's Vegan Bistro to succeed. Spending long hours together made for a relaxed, friendly relationship between everyone there.

At some point, Malik began to share aspects of his relationship with Tara, asking Latisha for her opinion. Nothing that was too big of a deal, and nothing too private. Things like, what did she think about the negative influence of friends? A hobby becoming an addiction? People being taken in by a shyster? Bit by bit, Malik revealed just enough for Latisha to paint a picture of what was happening: Tara's interest in past life regression was turning into an obsession; her spending was increasing; a ditzy friend whom Malik didn't like held too much influence; and Tara's behavior was becoming more unpredictable. Only recently she'd came home looking terrified, saying she'd been drowned as a witch. It really worried him. What if they didn't come out of it?

Latisha always listened with empathy. Sometimes she practiced techniques learned in acting classes from long ago, successfully prompting Malik to provide additional details, often saying more than he intended.

She now found herself standing on the sidelines watching a relationship as if it were her own reality TV.

You're too good for her, she kept thinking. *Leave.*

"If something starts between us, and they're just living together, that doesn't count as much as if they were married, right?" Latisha asked Akemi.

"What are you trying to say? It's not as bad if you break up a relationship because they're not married yet?"

"Sort of."

"I don't know... it doesn't seem right to me to break up a couple. Karma and all that. It can come back to hurt you."

"What if they're already broke? Or at least shaky....?"

"Broke would be different. How shaky?"

"Shakier than not."

"What if it was less shaky than you thought? But you still broke them up. Could you live with yourself?"

"I think so. It'd be different if they had kids."

"That *is* a plus," affirmed Akemi.

"Finally, we're getting somewhere." Like most people with their eyes set on a prize, Latisha fished for the answers she desired. "Really, I don't think he's that happy with her. He's always telling me things she's doing that he doesn't like. Maybe I'll just tell him how I feel. It's getting harder just being there."

"All I'm saying," Akemi counselled, "is be careful. I don't want to see you hurt."

Despite longing to tell Malik her feelings, bearing Akemi's words in mind, Latisha chose otherwise. She'd bide her time. Drop hints. Be subtle. Weeks passed by and the restaurant got busier due to unexpected publicity from The New York Post.

One night, as they were closing up, Malik unexpectedly asked:

"Hey, how about a drink before going home?"

"Sure, I'd love one."

He placed two glasses on the bar counter. Latisha watched as he tilted the bottle, and the plum-colored wine swirled inside the round glass.

"I need to share something with you," he said.

"Oh yeah?"

"You've been so good over the past year. Stood by me, Helped me. Listened to me."

"The feeling is mutual, Malik."

"It's meant a lot for me to get to know you."

"Me too." Latisha smiled cautiously, "I like you very much."

"Thank you."

"I think you're a very special guy."

"I want to show you something."

He pulled out a small box.

She stood there speechless.

Malik flipped open the lid.

Inside, nestled between the ruffles of pearl white silk, was a gold ring inlaid with a row of perfectly cut diamonds.

"It's beautiful."

He gave a broad smile.

"Do you think Tara will like it?"

She could feel her throat tighten. Nothing came out.

"Well?"

"She'll," she forced herself to cough, loosening up the muscles that had frozen stiff. "She'll love it. What woman wouldn't?"

"I had to show you." He beamed.

"Congratulations." Latisha smiled, tilting her head back to rush the wine down her raw throat, alcohol over an open wound.

When will it be my turn?

Akemi

Men.

She'd always liked them older: they seemed surer of themselves when compared to men her own age.

Akemi was weary of the ones trying to "find themselves," and wary of those who were too confident. When looking for a male, she applied The Goldilocks Rule: This bed's too soft, this bed's too hard, this bed's just right. She wanted someone who knew who they were, comfortable in their own skin - just right.

Gerry fit the bill.

Despite his quiet demeanor, he was sure of himself. He was funny, too. His dry sense of humor slipped out at the most unexpected moments, usually in sarcastic comments said with a straight face. Occasionally, a tiny curve on the side of his mouth betrayed Gerry's intent. Playful, more than smart-ass.

There were twenty-seven years between them.

The age difference made things more intriguing for them both. Gerry was interested in Akemi's future hopes and dreams. She wanted to learn of Gerry's life experiences and adventures while traveling the world, visiting places she yearned to see.

Since meeting Latisha years ago on the first day of an acting class, Akemi, and Latisha became fast friends and confidants. The assignment given by their creative-if-caustic professor was to develop an original performance based on a type of food rising in the oven. Latisha had portrayed a chocolate chip cookie that gently bubbled and melted on the tray, while Akemi enacted a cheese soufflé, rising light and airy. The professor singled them out as giving the best performances that day, heads above unleavened breads and misguided lasagnas. After class, high on his recognition, they chatted for the first time—and hadn't stopped since.

Like Latisha, Akemi had worked long and hard, auditioning for roles while supporting herself through a string of waitressing and bartending jobs. Along with so many other hopefuls who'd moved to the city, their freshness had faded, and their CVs were prone to hyperbole; they were filled with exaggerated descriptions of roles which made them seem more important than they were. They lived in a subsistence economy, cash in one hand, then out the other. Artists of all stripes were left standing on the same spot they'd been a decade ago, looking up at the billboards, imagining their own faces there.

Still, Akemi eked out enough of a living to rent her own five flight walk-up apartment in Williamsburg – it was the shape of a shoebox and only slightly larger.

Is this it? Is this really all there is?

Lately, this question had been circling in her mind. When did she begin questioning her life choices? She couldn't answer. Self-doubt had stealthily crept in, taking Akemi by surprise, making her grapple with insecurities she didn't know she had.

Just as she was taking stock, reassessing her life, Akemi crossed paths with Gerry.

"Last night I went on a date with a nice guy," she told Latisha.

"Go on."

"We were together for a couple of hours and there was a good vibe. It was almost like we skipped steps and fast-tracked to getting to know each other."

"Where'd you meet?"

"He was in the hotel bar at work, at a table, sitting by himself. I served him a drink and we began to chat. It was a quiet night, so he moved to the bar," she paused, looking for the words, and then just shook her head.

"What is it?"

"I don't know," she pondered out loud. "He had a kind of sadness in him."

"How do you mean?"

"Hard to say. Not a miserable expression, or a depressed look... it was more of a feeling I could pick up on. His aura, I suppose."

"So, what happened?"

"He pretty much talked with me until I closed the bar at two in the morning and then went back to his room."

"Did you go with him?"

"Those fast days are over." Akemi laughed. "But he asked when my night off was, and I told him the next day. He invited me to dinner, and I said yes."

"Sounds promising," Latisha winked. "What's he look like?"

"Mmmm... good question. I'd say...nice looking, but not what you'd call typically handsome. Tall-ish, brown eyes. White. Irish, I think. Or Scotch-Irish. McNamara's his last name."

"He has all his hair?"

"No, but it's close-cropped, so looks fine."

"If you say so."

"Don't discriminate. Bald men need love too. He does have a goatee, though."

"How old?"

"Fifty-nine."

"Girl, are you out of your mind? You're thirty-two. He's older than your father."

"I know. But I like him. I could do with something good in my life right now."

"Well, I'll say to you what you say to me," Latisha's sympathetic voice was undergirded by concern. "I don't want you to get hurt."

Several months had passed, Akemi and Gerry had been in touch with each other every day. His initial visit to the city had been for a job interview at a publishing house. As it transpired, he lived in Houston. Gerry had got the job and was currently shuttling back and forth, meeting team members from the company's division he'd oversee. He was also apartment hunting.

"I hope you'll move in with me," he'd said after a few weeks of knowing Akemi.

"It's important to get to know each other a bit more but I'm definitely open to the idea."

Do I want to wake up next to him every day? Sit across the table? Does he want a baby the way I do? I need to change my life but want to be sure Gerry's the one to do it with.

It was a couple of weeks after Gerry found the ideal apartment that Akemi got the callback.

"You got the part," the director said. "Congratulations."

Akemi jumped for joy, but soon found herself thinking about Gerry with an unexpected weightiness.

Have Your Cake and Eat It would mean a nine-month tour of major cities all around the country.

"What should I do?" she asked Latisha.

"I'm so jealous!" she said, obviously thrilled for her friend. "It's your turn! You've worked all your life for this opportunity. It's why you came to New York."

"I know, but I'm just starting with Gerry and it's been going so well. He's found an apartment overlooking Central Park and wants me to move in with him."

"Why can't you have the best of both worlds?"

"What do you mean?"

"You can tour, and Gerry can fly out on your days off."

"I wish. I'll be working long weekends and traveling most days off."

"Well... at least try. Do your best to make it work."

The play was about friends who worked in demanding jobs while juggling men and motherhood. A surprise success of the Broadway season two years earlier, only one of the four leads had agreed to sign on, leaving three vacant roles. It was a long shot for Akemi, who'd intermittently played minor to moderate roles in middling theaters.

Maybe my track record isn't as bad as I thought it was.

It would be a huge leap to go on the road in a steady job, the biggest commitment of her career to date.

Who'd have believed it? Just when I was going to give the whole fucking thing up...

"That's how life works, sometimes," Gerry said when she told him of the opportunity. "You should definitely do it. It's what you always wanted. Don't get me wrong, I'll miss you terribly. But it's only nine months," he assured her. "I think we can weather that."

She went.

The tour, so far, had been a moderate success. Akemi enjoyed the challenges of performing, and the nightly responsibility of giving her all to an appreciative audience. Her fellow actors were fun to be with. After each performance, the make-up and wigs came off and they headed to a local bar. She'd developed a tentative friendship with Phillip, who played her estranged husband. Akemi could tell that he liked her but played down his interest. Gerry called every night, and they took turns in sharing their days. She missed him, yet was grateful her plate was full, and she was finally doing what she loved. Each post-night session with the cast allowed them to indulge in their latest performance. They talked about their

116

inner processes and subtle changes they'd made, constantly refining their craft.

One night returning from their libations, they found the hotel elevator broken, requiring them to walk up the dimly lit emergency stairs. They all had a few more drinks than usual, with Akemi and Phillip lagging behind the others. It had been a particularly good performance that night, and Akemi was on a natural high. When Phillip leaned over and kissed her, she was not surprised. Nor was she that surprised at her own reaction, returning the kiss. They'd been simmering on low heat for a while, more than Akemi cared to acknowledge. She'd been down this street before - it wouldn't mean anything.

Akemi woke up the next morning to gentle snoring, Phillip's leg wrapped around hers, and sheets falling to the floor.

She felt her dry throat and instant regret.

What am I doing?

Slipping out of the bed, Akemi gathered her belongings and tiptoed down the hall to her own room. She stood with her back against the door.

I can't let that happen again.

She dialed Gerry's number.

"Good morning," she said as soon as he picked up.

"Good morning! Isn't this a little early for you in Phoenix?"

"Sorta. But I couldn't sleep. I just wanted to tell you that I love you."

117

"Awww. That's nice," he was a little taken aback. "It's been a little while since you've said it."

"Has it?" It was her turn to be surprised.

"Yes, it has. I love you too," he said.

"I mean, I know," she continued. "But now I *really* know."

"Are you okay? You sound a little different than usual. Did something happen?"

"No. Nothing," she responded. "Just missing you."

"See," Gerry assured. "I told you it would all be okay."

Gerry

It started almost imperceptibly, with small tremors that he could feel through the headboard of the hotel bed. Gerry was surprised at the level of accommodation provided by his potential employer. If this boutique hotel near Herald Square was a sign of things to come, they were surely on a fixed budget.

He was lying there relaxing, reading a memoir called *Lost and Found*. The real-life protagonist was a middle-aged man whose wife died unexpectedly. His world, now decimated, the man walked through the aftermath like a freak survivor of a nuclear attack.

Prone to hyperbole, perhaps. But I get it.

These feelings went on for years: the pleasure of life evaporated, leaving only a vacuum. Every move felt like the performance of existence. Then one day, a simple revelation occurred to the author. He had closed himself off from the world, creating a bubble as protection from further hurt and pain. While ensuring much needed safety and security, the bubble also caused numbness, for it meant no real feelings got in. Understanding this, the author reflected deeply, encouraging himself be open, even if cautiously, to what the universe might bring.

At first, Gerry ignored the tremors, concentrating harder on his book, until they became more pronounced, accompanied by muffled sounds. Then it dawned on him, the people in the next room were having sex. This was confirmed when he raised a hand to the headboard and felt the vibrations through his palm. Gerry put down his book on the bed, then returned his hand to the board, palm against wood, fingers splayed like a starfish.

119

The movement entering his fingertips was regular, rhythmic. It struck him that he was, in some strange way, now physically connected to the couple in the adjacent room as they made love. Part of Gerry urged himself to pull away, practicing restraint, permitting privacy. Another part of him marveled at the unexpected, sharing such an intimate moment with strangers, feeling an energy enter his body. Having sex was, after all, one of the most universal acts in the world.

What kind of couple were they? Gerry wondered. Deeply in love, consummating a physical desire, compelled to each other like magnets? Was it an affair, hidden from spouses, riding on heightened excitement of indulging in the forbidden? Or perhaps a monetary transaction between a lonely businessman and a call girl dreaming of a better life for her children? Were they young people with tight bodies and boundless energy? Middle-aged, larger in size, slightly sagging, seizing on a second wind to explore former pleasures from carefree days? Could they be an older couple who'd carried their torch for decades, still happy kindling the fire?

Hand remaining flat against the wood, Gerry felt his penis stir, unsure what to make of it.

Then Helen appeared in his mind. She had always been the sexiest woman he'd ever met.

One hand remained on the headboard as the other unbuttoned his pants.

They'd had a beautiful relationship. They made love in ways they'd never done before, surprised at their explorations, sometimes laughing, slightly embarrassed by their forthrightness in enjoying each other's bodies. With Helen, Gerry felt no limits. His wife had been lover, best friend, universe.

Now, roused by the anonymous couple next door, Gerry recalled some of his favorite memories of making love to

Helen. The time in Tuscany, hanging out their rented farmhouse window, high upon a secluded hill. In their kitchen, amid dinner preparation, seized by the sudden urge to possess each other. One of his absolute favorites, the first time they were naked together in bed. It was midday and snow falling softly outside as classical music played. Also, the countless times where one gently reached over in the middle of the night, knowing the exact places to touch.

The orgasm came quickly, weeping a slow ooze over his clenched fingers. At the same time, Gerry emitted an unfamiliar whimpering animal-like sound. Removing his other hand from the headboard, he felt tears roll out the corner of his eyes. Sex and sorrow were not meant for each other.

He would never forgive himself; he had been driving that day.

They were running late for work, Gerry anxious to arrive on time for an important meeting. Hastily pulling out from their driveway, he didn't see the other car coming. It was speeding, he'd later come to find out. All Gerry remembered before passing out was the bang, the sound of metal-on-metal and with the explosion of glass, bursting like a firework, thousands of tiny slivers spraying in all directions.

They'd been in such a hurry that Helen hadn't yet fastened her seat belt. The vehicle rammed into the passenger side of their car, smashing her head hard on the dashboard. The paramedics did their best to save her, but arriving at the hospital, she'd already succumbed to the trauma and was gone. Gerry, on the other hand, only suffered severe whiplash, with moderate cuts and bruises.

After the burial, Helen's family had stopped speaking to him. Thank goodness his own children, as distraught as they were, understood and forgave him.

He'd do anything to get Helen back.

It had been over two years, and Gerry thought of her every day. From the instant she died, depression moved into his heart, like a squatter making claim, refusing to leave. He'd come to accept the situation, making peace with his permanent resident.

Not wishing to wallow, something Gerry found easy to fall into, he rolled off the bed and headed to the bathroom. Now feeling a little hungry, a quick shower and some bar food were in order.

Ten minutes later, as he stepped out of his room into the hallway, Gerry heard the click of another door opening. His neighbors emerged. Two middle-aged women dressed casually in jeans and t-shirts. Mystery solved. He chastised himself for not having considered other alternatives.

"Good evening," the one with curly hair said.

"Good evening," he responded, knowing they were unaware of their connection.

The three of them stood by the elevator. Was he imagining it, or did it feel a little awkward?

"Weather's been warm today," said the one with a gap in her teeth, puncturing the air.

"Yes," he answered. "Off to see a show?"

"Tomorrow," she replied. "Tonight, we're off to our favorite restaurant in Chinatown. You?"

"I'll be happy with a quick bite and an early night. Here for business more than pleasure, unfortunately."

"That's a shame. There's so many things to do."

"Yup. Actually, I have job interview tomorrow. If I get lucky, it'll be my turn to do the fun things here."

Their polite conversation continued as the elevator arrived and descended to the lobby. On reaching the ground floor, the gap-toothed woman said, "Nice talking with you. Enjoy your quiet night." The curly-haired one added, "Good luck tomorrow."

He was disappointed with the menu, standard fare, mainly burgers.

"Hi, my name is Akemi and I'll be serving you tonight. What can I get you?"

"Akemi... that's a pretty name."

She noticed something different in his voice. So many men wanted to flirt, often using the exact same line. But this time it was sincere and, at the same time, a little wistful.

"Japanese. Means bright dawn."

"Wow. I was right," he glanced up from the menu. "I'll have a pastrami on rye, no pickle, and a pint of Scottish ale."

"Sounds good. I'll be back. We're short-staffed tonight so I'm tending bar, too. Apologies in advance if there's a slight delay."

Nice voice too, he thought. "Don't worry, no rush."

A football match was playing on several screens. Gerry feigned interest, watching figures chase each other up and down the field in pursuit of the ball. It was easier to look at the TV than other people, who seemed to be in couples or groups wherever he went. He'd become master of telephone Sudoku,

123

and adept at turning book pages while eating. Such were the habits of being solo.

On finishing his meal, Gerry started heading back to the room, but something held him back. Instead, he turned around and climbed on a stool at the bar. Contrary to Akemi's warnings of potential delays, it happened to be a slow night. Once the diners left, the bar was empty except for them, affording the unexpected opportunity for a chat. As it turned out, she was an actress who worked tables and bars to pay the rent.

Gerry found himself engaging in a way that he hadn't for some time. Akemi's easy-going manner, her ability to effortlessly transition from one topic to another, drew him in. They began to share elements of their life stories. Before long, it felt as if they'd known one other for a lot longer.

During their conversation, Gerry became aware of a desire to look closely at Akemi, discretely studying her in subtle ways. Simultaneously, he was becoming more self-conscious, for she seemed to be doing the same thing to him. Although a lot younger than him, Gerry noticed Akemi had a level of maturity not seen in many people his own age. By the end of the night, he'd surprised himself by asking her to have dinner the following night and could hardly believe when she accepted.

Am I actually doing this? He asked himself, shocked by his audaciousness. *What would Helen say?*

"Best of luck tomorrow," Akemi said as she closed up the bar. "I'll say a little prayer."

"I'm glad it's at midday," Gerry replied. "I've had more to drink than I usually do."

"Give me your phone and I'll put in my number," she instructed. "I'll have to be discrete. They don't like employees fraternizing with customers."

Back in his room, Gerry felt wired, unable to sleep. While chatting at the bar, he'd spotted the women from his neighboring room as they entered the hotel. Passing by on the way to the elevator, the curly-haired one noticed him and gave a friendly wave. The one with the gap in her teeth called over, "Don't burn the midnight oil. Big day tomorrow." Now, he imagined, they'd be asleep in each other's arms, warm skin against warm skin. One of the best feelings in the world. Even better was knowing you're not alone in the middle of the night.

Trust. He missed it all so much.

Propping a pillow behind his head, Gerry picked up his copy of *Lost and Found,* opening where he left off.

The author began to describe how he took chances, calling it his wake up call to the world again.

Unable to concentrate, Gerry closed the book and lay his head on the pillow. He opened his phone and looked at Akemi's number.

Maybe.

He tried to sort through his feelings about what had just happened. For the first time since Helen, he'd sensed an emotional connection with a woman. Fragile, but there.

Gerry had felt it.

That tiny knot of nerve endings, buried deep down.

It scared him.

125

He knew the feeling.

It was a spark.

Nancy

As Nancy lay on the bed, she watched Lyndsey through the open bathroom door, wearing only a black bra and underwear, curling her hair with heated tongs.

"Have I ever told you how sexy you are?" Nancy asked.

"Pretty much every day."

It was part of their routine, going back and forth, with predictable lines.

"Will you marry me?"

"Already did."

"Do you ever get tired of using those things?"

"Nope.

"Don't they damage your hair? I read something once that said to avoid them like the plague."

"They're fine if used responsibly and in moderation."

The response summed up Lyndsey. Careful. Measured. Confident.

Sixteen years together.

Leaving the suburbs of Albany for the weekend, they came to the city in celebration of their tenth wedding anniversary. As soon as their hotel room door was closed, Nancy and Lyndsey indulged themselves with abandon. In giving mutual pleasure, the bed had rocked steadily, knocking against the wall.

Afterwards, Lyndsey asked, "Do you think they heard us next door?"

"Nah. Probably no one there."

"You're still a wild woman after all these years."

"Look who's talking." Nancy raised her brows. "You sound like we've got two feet in the grave."

"Are we getting buried together?"

"Now that you've mentioned it, I don't see why not."

They continued to banter for a while, happily ensconced in their own world, before Lyndsey chastised:

"Get your derriere out of bed, m'lady. There's a big city out there waiting for us. Put your clothes on, and we'll walk to Chinatown."

"I need a shower first."

"Agreed."

While standing in the hallway, locking their door, they noticed a man leaving the adjacent room. It was occupied after all.

He must have heard, Nancy thought, embarrassed, now standing next to him in silence, waiting for the elevator. Lyndsey broke the ice with him, innocuously mentioning the weather.

God, she's good at making small talk.

Nancy had always been a shy person. As a child, she'd loved learning in school but hated the social dynamics of classrooms, hallways, and lunchrooms. A bit of a tomboy, she endured teasing for preferring to wear pants and sporting short-cut hair. Confused, at first Nancy thought she wanted to be a boy, but then figured out she just liked things that were more associated with boys. Wearing sneakers. Watching wrestling. Shooting hoops. In her case, usually solo. Just as she'd shown no interest in dressing up dolls, Nancy shuddered at the thought of cheerleading. Pretty much a loner, she remained awkward in a world not configured with Nancy in mind. Teenage years were spent keeping a low profile as other boys and girls flirted, making awkward moves for each other.

Her parents initially had different hopes but any misgivings were short-lived. Once they'd accepted Nancy for who she was, they ceased suggesting she grow her hair longer, wear a little make up to "take the pale off," and choose flowery summer dresses. Instead, her parents grew to appreciate Nancy's close-cropped hair, telling themselves it made her appear "pixie-ish" not butch. They let her choose sturdy sneakers and comfortable shoes, shaking their heads *no* when shop assistants brought anything stylish and impractical, trying to head them off at the pass. Unsurprising, jeans were Nancy's preferred fashion choice. So easy to match with t-shirts.

Asexual. That's what Nancy thought she was on leaving her Far Rockaway high school, heading off to college in Buffalo. Researching asexuality as if it were a curious phenomenon separate from herself, Nancy didn't know what all the fuss was about. She never felt the urge to have sexual relations with boys or girls and rarely thought about it. She would rather focus on her studies. And so, in shy Nancy style, she went through her bachelor's and master's degrees without a kiss or a touch.

She'd always had fair, smooth skin, flecked with freckles, making her look younger than she was. Still preferring a short haircut, and opting for no makeup, Nancy looked somewhat androgynous, and was easily mistaken for a young man.

Having a fairly flat chest and slim hips also helped give this impression. While well aware that her looks didn't conform to most representations of women on television, in film, and throughout the pages of glossy magazines, Nancy was still happy. Occasionally seeing women like herself in malls, on buses, or in coffee shops confirmed that others also refused the pressures of artifice, instead, taking comfort in who they were.

Being a lesbian came late. Mid-thirties to be exact. In the form of Lyndsey Hammersmith, a doctoral student a few years younger.

Nancy had been a reference librarian in Syracuse University for a while. She liked the genteel ambience in quiet rows of book stacks, silent study rooms, and lowered voices at reference desks. The world, generally speaking, had lost the desire and ability to tell the truth. Within a horror-show of nonstop technological demands, impersonality, and copious amounts of inane information, Nancy treasured the library as a sanctuary where she felt nourished and could nourish others. To her, there was nothing better than helping people look for specific sources of knowledge. It was her purpose in life.

The day that Lyndsey walked up to the reference desk signaled the moment that life thereafter would be divided into BL (Before Lyndsey) and AL (After Lyndsey).

It was as simple as that.

The voice. It was Lyndsey's voice that Nancy noticed first. It sounded full of patience and kindness, no matter what she was saying. The lips too, full, slightly puffy, and a gap between her two front teeth. There was something about that gap. Nancy searched to see if she could put her finger on what it was. Under her breath she murmured, "It's sexy."

Nancy recalled The Wife of Bath from Chaucer's *Canterbury Tales*, described as "gat-toothed," Old English for gate-toothed. It was a curious detail that had always stuck in Nancy's mind, for in Chaucer's day it was a sign of lasciviousness.

Lyndsey informed Nancy that she was studying Women and Gender Studies.

"What attracted you to that subject?" Nancy heard herself ask, surprised at her own directness.

"I'm interested in changing the historical record of women's contributions to knowledge in particular and society in general."

"Well, you have your work cut out for you."

Lyndsey noticed Nancy's natural reticence in conversation, how she visibly pushed herself to engage.

"I also like to look at how gender intersects with social class, race, religion, sexual orientation—the opportunities some people are afforded, and others denied," continued Lyndsey. "Stuff like that." She smiled, her gap on full display, mesmerizing as a hypnotist's watch.

"Wow."

"Actually, what I'm working on at the moment is a research project about shyness and librarians. It seems there's a correlation."

"Really?"

"Yes. I'm wondering if you'd be willing to be interviewed?"

"I am not sure, I—"

"It can be relaxed. Over a cup of coffee."

Nancy's face betrayed a subtle battle as she wrestled with what to say next.

"Um, okay, I guess."

They met the next evening at a local coffee shop and talked about a variety of things—the notion of herstory vs. history, overlooked female inventors, best ways to combine terms for an advanced search, and favorite books. Lyndsey loved Stein's *The Autobiography of Alice B. Toklas* and Atwood's *The Handmaid's Tale*. Nancy favored Lee's *To Kill a Mockingbird* and Shelley's *Frankenstein*.

"Interesting. They're all female authors," Lyndsey observed. "You like the classics, then."

"I do," confessed Nancy. "When will we begin the interview?"

Lyndsey began to giggle.

"Why are you laughing?"

"I said I was doing a research project on shy librarians so I could get you out for a cup of coffee."

"Oh," Nancy was surprised. "I see."

"I thought you'd read between the lines."

Nancy sat bemused for a moment before saying:

"Looks like I didn't even see the lines."

Then she looked at Lyndsey, who was still smiling. Parted lips, pearly teeth, sexy gap. It all clicked into place.

I get it now.

What took me so long?

They relived this scene, as they had done many times before, reminiscing at their anniversary dinner. Having strolled down Fifth Avenue to Washington Square Park, they'd wound their way through Soho and Little Italy, ending up on Mott Street in Chinatown at one of their favorite restaurants, *Wok and Roll*. The original pull had been the combination of delicious Chinese food with a soundtrack of 50s music. Here, they feasted on sweetcorn and crab soup, spring rolls, Peking duck, and sautéed scallops, while listening to Little Richard and Elvis.

Yes, life is good.

Nancy couldn't believe how fast their years together had passed, wishing she could press her finger on the pause button of life, savoring the luxury of time. Lyndsey had brought focus and meaning, joy and pleasure in ways that exceeded Nancy's wildest imagination. She loved her with every fiber of her being.

How lucky am I?

The fortune cookies arrived, along with thinly sliced oranges, glistening with freshness.

"You go first," instructed Nancy. It was another ritual in their shared world.

"Okay," said Lyndsey, reaching for the plate. "Let's see what I get."

Using both thumbs, she cracked open the cookie and pulled out the slip of paper.

"The greatest risk is not taking one," she read, raising her eyebrows. "Well, I can't argue with that," pursing her lips toward Nancy. "Now you."

Nancy picked up the remaining fortune cookie, crushing it in the palm of her hand with calculated hyperbole, before plucking the words of wisdom like wheat from chaff.

"Wow!" Lyndsey gasped in mock admiration, "Conan the Librarian."

"It says...," Nancy squinted a little, having forgotten her reading glasses. "'If you refuse to accept anything but the best, you often get it.'"

"Amen, honey," Lyndsey replied. "Story of your life, eh?" She winked.

"It could also go the other way," offered Nancy. "I mean, if people are too fussy, they could end up with nothing."

"Trust you to see it that way," said Lyndsey playfully. "All in all, I think mine trumps yours. Gotta take risks sometimes. If you don't, things pass you by. That's why I asked you to be interviewed."

"And that's how I knew when the best thing came along."

"Touché!"

Afterwards, enjoying the night air, and feeling the need to walk off their food, they decided to slowly zig zag back to their hotel on foot. As they walked up Fifth Avenue they admired store windows displaying designer suits, dazzling gowns, and hand-stitched Italian shoes; Nancy marveled at such luxuries while wondering about the people who bought them. To her, material goods were dangled in front of everyone with the promise of making a person look better, feel better, which often translated to *being better* than those around them. Items for sale created a fraudulent exterior of self-worth, favored over something deeper, cultivated within. Each season meant fresh new designs, creating a consumer treadmill of customers always running without ever arriving.

Sitting on the sidewalk beneath the endless displays of symbolic wealth were people at the opposite end of the consumer spectrum. They'd fallen through the cracks due to genuine misfortune, simple bad luck, or poor choices. Tucked into store doorways for the night, some asked for money from passersby, while others sat silently with a sign noting they were a Vietnam Vet or a single mother who'd recently lost her job and apartment. Several had a dog who evoked more sympathy in some passers-by than their downtrodden owners. Nancy thought of these people as the "invisibles" of society, ghostly presences in plain sight who people chose to look through, preferring not to see.

But *she* saw them. It pained Nancy to bear witness. She felt part of the problem, by simply existing in a society where people didn't care enough for each other. To assuage her guilt, and help with a meal, she always kept five-dollar bills in her back pocket. As Lyndsey stopped to admire a window full of watches, Nancy noticed an old man sitting hunched in the doorway, surrounded by black garbage bags bulging with the remnants of his life's possessions. His beard was long, hair unkempt, and his eyes looking off into some other place. A sign on a square of tattered cardboard read, "Homeless. Please spare money for food."

Reaching into the back pocket of her jeans, Nancy plucked out a five-dollar bill and handed it to the man.

"There you go, buddy."

He reached out his hand and nodded a silent thank you. She wished she could do the same thing for every homeless person she passed, but also knew it was *not the answer*. Still,

135

it was a modest gesture that provided tangible support for someone. The accompanying guilt she always felt was partly rooted in gratitude for not being in their shoes.

There but for the grace of God go I.

On their way through the lobby of the hotel Nancy noticed the man from the room next door sitting at the bar talking to the bartender. She gave him a wave. Lyndsey, remembering his job interview the next day, cautioned him not to stay up too late. Just as the elevator came, another couple joined them. A man and woman, not drunk, but noticeably merry, began chatting to them about what a great place New York City was.

"On holiday?" Lyndsey ventured.

"Yes," said the woman. "I love it here. Third time."

"We love it, too," Nancy replied.

Imperceptible to the others, Nancy noticed a slight shift in the man's demeanor, as if something blurred had suddenly come into focus. As the woman and Lyndsey shared plans for the next day, the man stared straight ahead although Nancy could feel him take stock of her with his peripheral vision. The elevator stopped.

"This is our floor," declared Lyndsey.

"Nice talking to you," said the woman.

"You too," Lyndsey said as she stepped into the hallway.

"Goodnight," Nancy nodded.

As the elevator doors were closing, Nancy heard the man say:

136

"Have a good night," before lowering his voice, assuming she was out of earshot, "eating pussy."

The doors closed.

"Did you hear what he said?" Nancy asked Lyndsey.

"No. What did he say?"

After telling her, Nancy felt a flush of anger. It had been so quick. She'd wanted to say something back to him, but didn't know what, other than it being *something*, if only to challenge his sense of entitlement to speak that way.

"He probably enjoys doing it himself," shrugged Lyndsey. "And if he doesn't, he has no idea what he's missing."

Nancy mulled it over.

"You're right," she said walking down the hallway. "Fuck him."

"No thanks."

"Amen to that," said Nancy, closing the room door behind her. "Now come over here and give me a real kiss."

Arthur

I can't remember the time when I stopped talking. Then again, I don't have much use for time or talking these days. It wasn't really a conscious decision to protest something, like a hunger strike. I just didn't see the point in doing it anymore. If someone gives me money, I nod or raise my hand a little as a gesture of thanks. That's enough.

I like it better in my own world with my own thoughts. Feels safer.

Through the day I sit at my street corner. Let it all go by. Sometimes I look at the ground. Other times I watch the people. Most of them are always rushing to get where they need to be. Once there, they're already planning to rush to the next place, heads filled with plans, lists, things to do.

I know because I lived in that world.

Yesterday, I decided to talk for a while. It came back easily, like riding a bicycle. Two young people wanted to interview me. I felt kind of sorry for them. I'd seen both approach a few others nearby, but no one wanted to be bothered. The poor things started to look frustrated and a bit disappointed.

They had clipboards and pens and wore yellow jackets with the name of their project, HOTS. Stands for Homeless Off The Streets, they told me. Said their names were Theresa and Imani. Part of a new project by the city to find out how people came to live on the streets. I could see they had real concern. I can tell how people are by the way they look at me. It's in the eyes. Always in the eyes. Of course, the majority don't look. They keep on walking to their homes, offices, bars, gyms, subway stops... Passing by as fast as they can, eyes straight ahead or glued to their phones. Those who do look

138

*fall into three main categories that sort of represent the
human race.*

1. Those who care:
*These people recognize you as a human being. No matter
that you wear dirty clothes and have become accustomed to
how bad you smell, they still look at you with feelings of
compassion. There's a recognizable sadness when our eyes
meet and mirror being human, just like themselves, only in a
wretched state. They fear the unimaginable, that this could
perhaps be themselves one day. Sitting alone on a sidewalk,
bereft of love, family, and support. Someone who has fallen
between the cracks of all that is familiar and found
themselves far from the crowd and a normal existence. Lost.*

2. Those who are on the fence:
*These people know you are human too and perceive that
flaws have usually tilted the scales away from you.
Otherwise, how did you get here? They weigh pity and
empathy in equal measure with a pendulum swinging
unpredictably between them. Of course, they feel sorry for
you and would hate to be in your position. At the same time,
they silently convey that you've let them down in some
strange way by being irresponsible, not doing your part to
ensure that all of society is functioning. They know that while
not everyone's given the same opportunities in life,
everyone's supposed to take what they've been given and
somehow make it work. No matter what, you can pull
yourself up by your bootstraps. To them, you're a reminder
that not everyone makes it, and some of that's just the luck of
the draw, simply how life is—filled with winners and losers.*

3. Those who don't care:
*These people refuse to recognize you as fully human. They
don't even want to acknowledge your existence. If you exert
yourself in any capacity, including appealing to them for
financial support or food, they're either afraid, angry, even
both. You've lost your right to be considered equal. Instead,
you've been placed not even at the margins, but outside of*

them. It's your own fault, and now you're your own responsibility, so don't bother me. You're an affront to everyone else. The lowest of the low. An eyesore. A stain. Something to step around, like garbage, asking: Why should I care about you if you've already given up on yourself?

I know. because when on the other side of the equation— as the viewer, not the viewed—I once shifted among all three categories. I remember walking briskly to work, briefcase in hand, mentally prepared and ready for another day of scheduled patients. I did my best with their crumbling teeth, rotting gums, and pungent halitosis. I made sure to keep them calm during root canals and crown installations. I wanted my patients to be satisfied and I cared about doing a good job. After all, everyone wants to have a confident smile. It's a birthright in America. If you have the misfortune not to be blessed with a good set of teeth, they can always be bought.

Theresa and Imani seemed genuinely concerned about me. It had been a long time since that had happened. Someone standing close, looking me directly in the eye. Theresa told me HOTS is an operation with two objectives: the first is to come to know the real stories of people on the streets and how they got there, so support systems can be made stronger. The second is to try and get them on their feet again, help them transition back into society.

The questions they kept asking took me back and got me thinking again about the past. It's a place I'd rather not go, but they were so nice that I decided to share a few things. Like me, they cared about doing a good job and definitely belonged in the category of people who care.

You know, it's easier to be in the present. The future is not worth speculating about, as anything can happen. It doesn't pay to think about it too much, otherwise a whole lot of

140

worry sets in and that's all you do—worry about all of the possibilities. It's endless.

That's why it's easier to be in the present. Just to be. In the now. Sunup, sundown, through the night. One day at a time. Know which soup kitchens are open and what time they serve. Where to go to the bathroom. How to keep warm. Where to get water.

Everything stripped down to the basics of survival.

When they asked, I told them it all started with a parking ticket I forgot to pay. The thing had escalated to way beyond the original fine into hundreds of dollars. I was on my way to the courthouse in Staten Island, where I lived since I'd been married. I needed to explain that my wife Evelyn had left me without warning. This had made me very depressed, for weeks, months. I hadn't been leaving the house much, I wasn't able to. I couldn't shake the depression and let certain things slide, this fine being one of them. But on the way to see the judge I had an accident, and the car was towed away. I never saw it again. There was also the rent, gas, electricity, credit cards. Things piled on top of each other. My associates at our practice were kind at first, full of concern. But when I couldn't keep up with my responsibilities, they let me go. One came to visit me a few times, but after a while, she stopped. Her life—like so many others—was just so busy. Rushing. Working. Eating. Sleeping.

Before then I'd already had debts from my daughter Julie's medical complications. Even with some insurance, the price of treatments had grown to a considerable degree. Evelyn and I had warned her about drugs, but she had it in her head to do things the way she wanted. We'd gotten Julie treatment, but she kept relapsing. This always happened. Then one day she took a trip too many and... never came back. Or at least her mind never did. Her body hung in for a while. Quite a while, actually, before it finally gave out. All of our savings went into taking care of her. We sold the house

141

and moved into a much smaller apartment. Everything went on Julie.

When she died, Evelyn and I were heartbroken. Our only baby gone, we kept asking ourselves: Where did we go wrong?

Evelyn cried day and night for months, saying "This is not supposed to happen," over and over, bewildered and betrayed by her own expectations of life. It wasn't in the script. Our grief, instead of uniting us, propelled us in different directions; we left each other far behind as we tried to find a way forward. I came to realize, no matter how close a relationship had been, it was common for parents' who'd lost a child to watch, immobilized from the sidelines, as their marriage disintegrated in plain view.

Yes, Evelyn left.

After that I could feel myself slipping further into quicksand, and while trying my best, couldn't seem to do anything about it. Once I'd lost the apartment and car, and the little money remaining in my bank account was seized for nonpayment of taxes owed, I stood on the street with only the clothes I wore. I hadn't given up by then and went to government offices, standing in long lines, taking numbers, waiting patiently, given forms, sent to more offices for more numbers, more lines, more forms. It was exhausting, and I...sort of... went under.

I know I should've fought harder, waited longer, spoken up. But I was exhausted from the last few years. So instead, I sat in some government office, unable to move.

"Sir, we're closing now. You have to leave."

"Sir, you have to leave."

"Sir, I will have to call security."

"Security!"

I found myself on the street again, bewildered at how my once coveted life—wife, family, job—running smoothly along the tracks of normalcy had suddenly left the security of its rails, tumbling into a place I could never fully imagine.

Over and over, I found myself on the street.

And this is where I've stayed.

For years now.

Since I gave up trying to make it all work.

It didn't make any sense. Nothing much made sense anymore.

I shared all of this with the kids asking questions and they told me about some new places in a nearby neighborhood, programs to get people back on their feet.

"I am so sorry to hear what happened to you," Theresa sympathized. "You've dealt with a lot."

"You should come to the Center one day," Imani encouraged. "There will be people to talk to, they'll see if they can find a place for you to live permanently." She seemed sincere, not matter of fact like some I've seen doing this outreach stuff.

"Thank you, Arthur," Theresa said, using my own name, something I hadn't heard in a long time. "It's been very helpful talking with you."

Sweet girl. Reminds me a little bit of my Julie.

"If you know any of these other guys," Theresa nodded her head in the direction of a cluster of people, "Do us a favor and tell them we're okay to talk to, will you?"

I nodded yes.

"Take care of yourself." Imani waved at me. "We'll be back around this way soon."

But I think I'll go back to not talking instead.

All those memories have made me feel a bit strange.

The sidewalk is a little cold, so I put corrugated cardboard beneath me. At night I found a new spot in the doorway of a watch store on Fifth Avenue. It's pretty safe and the cops leave me alone. I have to move when the manager comes in the morning. My sign is simple, asking for spare change to buy food. It's short, so people can read it as they pass by. At least the ones who look down.

Here's one now, slowly coming toward me. She's reaching out her hand with a five dollar note.

"There you go, buddy," she says.

Category one. I can see it in her eyes. She looks at me and gives a smile, but I know she's really sad, if only for that moment, before she goes back into her own life.

"Ready, Lyndsey?" She asked the woman she's with who was looking at watches in the store window.

They took each other's hand and continued walking.

Funny how times have changed.

Theresa

Theresa still missed her mother. It had been eleven years since she had seen her.

As she combed her shoulder-length shiny brown hair in the mirror, Theresa noticed her face was so pale it looked anemic, and she made a mental note to get more sun. Her small, dark eyes appeared tired, almost quizzical, squinting as if it was someone else staring back at her rather than her own reflection. Most of Theresa's peers at New York University had tired eyes, too, but for a different reason. They were partying every night, exploring the city with fake IDs bought in Times Square, suddenly aging from nineteen to twenty-one, with a laminated photograph to prove it. Now they had the key to the kingdom of Manhattan's endless bars and nightclubs. In contrast, Theresa's tiredness came from long days in which she juggled demanding classes, worked with the homeless population, traveled an hour each way on a crowded Brooklyn subway line, and took care of her aging grandmother in their small apartment. She told herself, *it'll all be worth it.* Studying psychology would eventually ensure a job as a family counselor or social worker.

"Need anything before I leave for class, Grandma?" Theresa asked, inserting her laptop into a backpack, along with her yellow jacket labeled with HOTS on the back. She noticed how much older her grandma, Rosa, looked these days—gray and stooped, with a milky-white cataract forming in one eye.

"No, sweetheart, I'm fine," said Rosa.

"Remember, this is one of my long days."

"What's that Lucia?"

Theresa raised her voice and spoke slowly, "It's me, Theresa, not Lucia. I won't be home until about nine tonight."

"That's right, I know. I know," Rosa said.

As she closed the apartment door, Theresa could feel the anxiety swirl inside her, creating a tight knot in her chest. Rosa's memory was deteriorating faster than Theresa wanted to admit. Her grandmother had started repeating the same questions, whether it be a random remembrance from the distant past or a current concern.

"Did I ever tell you about my sister, Luisa, who drowned when we were at the beach?"

"All my father's family died in the war. You know that, right?"

"It's a shame all politicians are criminals. What do you think?"

Such statements, once repeated days apart, became a daily occurrence, even hourly, and now, sometimes within a few minutes of each other.

"Can you bring me some honey when you come back?"

"Yes Grandma, you've asked me five times already," Theresa responded in a firm but kind voice.

"Oh, I have? I don't remember."

For Theresa, the worst part was when her grandmother mistook her for her mother, Lucia. It gave rise to all sorts of feelings like silt dredged up from a riverbed, spiraling in all directions before settling back down again.

On the train into the city, Theresa often pictured her mother's face as clear as if she'd seen it yesterday.

146

(Continued in Volume 2)

About the Author

Born in Newcastle, England, David J. Connor is a writer, artist, and educator who lives in New York City. His interests include story-telling and personal narratives within educational research, and designing book covers for colleagues. He has published ten books, including an autoethnographic memoir *Contemplating Dis/ability in Schools and Society: A Life in Education* (Lexington Press) and the soon to be released *How Teaching Shapes our Thinking about Disabilities: Stories from the Field* (Peter Lang Publishers), co-edited with Beth Ferri.

He can be reached at davidjohnconnor.djc@gmail.com